Dear Reader,

Being a teenager is a special time in everyone's life. And *Just for Us* books are written especially for teenage girls, to help make this time even more special.

I wish I'd had these books when I was younger. Each one of them is filled with all kinds of facts, tips, and ideas that really make sense. And they deal with all the things that teenage girls worry about. Some of the books are about how to get along with boys, your friends and family. Others help you learn how to figure out your emotions and even how to get along better with yourself! And still others show you how to look your beautiful best.

Maybe some of the problems that come up in these books will remind you of problems that have come up in your own life. Maybe some of the solutions will help you head off a crisis. And maybe some of the tips will help you meet someone special.

If you have comments about *Just for Us* books, or if you would like to suggest future titles, you can write to me at the address below. I'd love to hear from you because you're a very important part of *Just for Us*.

I'm thrilled to be introducing this wonderful new series. I hope you enjoy reading them, and I wish you the very best teen years ahead.

Sincerely,

Jill Whelan
c/o Pinnacle Books, Inc.,
1430 Broadway
New York,New York 10018

The JUST FOR US series from Pinnacle Books

JUST FOR US
JUST FOR US: BODY MAKEOVERS
JUST FOR US: YOUR CHANGING EMOTIONS
JUST FOR US: DATING

JUST FOR US

JILL WHELAN

PINNACLE BOOKS NEW YORK

JUST FOR US

An original Pinnacle Books edition, published for the first time anywhere.

First printing/September 1985

ISBN: 0-523-42572-4
Can. ISBN: 0-523-43522-3

Cover photo by John Cahoon/Outline

Printed in the United States of America

PINNACLE BOOKS, INC.
1430 Broadway
New York, New York 10018

9 8 7 6 5 4 3 2 1

CONTENTS

Introduction

BEING A TEENAGER can be the most exciting time of your life. Right? Well, sometimes. On the other hand the teen years can be the absolute worst time anyone can imagine.

We've all had moments when it seemed that everything was going wrong. Remember when that guy you liked dropped by unexpectedly one Saturday afternoon? Your hair was a mess, you had no makeup on, and your little brother had just pushed you past the point of no return with his creepy comments. Of course, that was the very instant he walked in—just in time to hear you screaming like a crazy person. Embarrassed wasn't the word for it! It was one of those terrible moments when you wished you could make time run backward and start the scene over. I remember plenty of embarrassing or scary or painful times. And there are lots more that I've managed to forget.

Does that surprise you? Sometimes people think that because I've been appearing on a television series since I was eleven years old, my life must be completely different from that of other girls my age. They believe I didn't have the same kinds of experiences and feelings and problems as other kids. But I did—and I still do.

Naturally my daily schedule *was* different, but my feelings about myself and my relationships with my family and friends went through the same ups and downs as anyone else's. I guess that's just part of being a teenager.

Everyone says that the years between childhood and adulthood are bound to be rough. That makes sense when you think about it. As teenagers, we all have to go through the often painful process of finding out who we are, where we fit in, and even what we want. This is hard to do—there are so many new choices to be made and new experiences to deal with. Lots of times you feel as if you don't even know the right questions to ask and you wouldn't recognize the right answer if it slapped you in the face.

Knowing that just about every teenager is going through the same crazy time you are helps a little; at least you know you're not alone. But realizing that your friends are feeling as weird and confused as you are doesn't tell you what to do about it.

I was lucky to have lots of people around who cared about me and tried to help me when I was confused or upset. It probably wasn't easy for them. And I didn't always follow their advice. I had to find things out on my own. I guess we all have to do that—that's how we discover what works for each of us. But often hearing about someone else's experiences can give you some clues about your own. That's why I'm glad to have the chance to tell you how I'm getting through my own teen years.

Chapter 1

Will the Real Jill Whelan Please Stand Up?

I GUESS WE all wonder what other people think of us. When I started at my new school here in Los Angeles, I was really nervous and scared, but I didn't know why. Now I realize that I was worried about whether or not I'd be accepted the same way I was in my old school. Would I make new friends who would like me as much as my old friends did? Would I do as well in class here as I had in my old school? Would I fit in here?

SEEING YOURSELF THROUGH OTHER PEOPLE'S EYES

As we become teenagers we all go through phases of worrying about what people think of us. When you consider it, this is pretty understandable. When we were little, we were used to taking our parents' word for the fact that we were cute kids in every way, and besides, we were too busy playing to care much about anyone else's opinions.

But a lot of things seem to change as we enter the teen years. The world seems to get bigger and more complicated because we're getting older and learning about other people's values and ideas. And our feelings are changing too. Teenagers begin to question their family's ways of doing things, although as younger children we wouldn't even have thought about this. Many teenagers find that they are growing away from their old friends and finding new friends who may have different attitudes about all kinds of things. And as we get a little older we start being interested in boys!

All these changes can make you feel as if you've become a completely different person. Of course, you really haven't, but it's true that you are not exactly the same as you were when you were a kid. And so sometimes you might start to wonder—will all those people who liked you a lot when you were younger still like you now that you have changed in certain ways? Do you still like them? Do you even like yourself? At times it's hard to answer that question, because at times you don't feel sure of who you are anymore.

SELF-CENTERED OR JUST SELF-CONSCIOUS?

I bet you've had people say to you about a million times, "You teenagers are so self-centered—why can't you think about anything but yourselves?"

These people are right in a way—we do think about ourselves a lot of the time. How can you help doing that when you're going through so many changes in almost every aspect of your life? There are so many new things to think through and figure out at this point in your life. But what people don't understand is that most of us would give anything to *not* think about ourselves all the time! It would be great to just relax and stop worrying about what other people think about us and what we think about ourselves.

Now that I'm older, I'm not so terribly self-conscious anymore, but I sure was when I was younger. When I first started working on TV, I commuted to Los Angeles every week from a town in northern California called Livermore—a really neat town—near San Francisco. I was still living in Livermore and I was enrolled in school there, but the show was filmed in Los Angeles, so my mom and I were in airports quite a lot.

It seemed to me that everyone in the whole place was staring at me all the time. I used to scrunch down in my seat and hide my face behind a book. And I was really nervous—I was sure that some of the men were just waiting for my mom to leave me alone while she bought a newspaper or something, and then they would kidnap me!

Sounds pretty dumb, don't you think? I realize now that while a few people really were looking at me because they had seen me on TV, other people probably weren't paying any attention to me at all—they were too busy hoping the plane wouldn't be late! But at that time of my life I was so self-conscious, I was sure everyone was staring at me.

You might think that because I've been on a TV show since I was eleven, I wouldn't be self-conscious at all. But like anyone else, I have certain things that I've felt embarrassed about or that I've been sure everyone was whispering and laughing about behind my back.

One thing I worried about for absolutely ages was getting my period. I was one of those girls who didn't start to menstruate until I was almost fourteen, and it seemed to me that everyone else I knew had already started, and I was the only girl my age in the whole world who hadn't. I just knew they were all either laughing at me or feeling sorry for me, and I used to pray every night, "Please let me get my period!"

I remember one day I was in the locker room changing clothes for gym class and I happened to notice that there was a spot of blood on this other girl's underpants. I guess she saw me looking and when she realized what had happened, she said in this really bored voice, "Oh, hey, thanks for noticing—I must have just got my period. What a drag, you know?"

I wanted to cry. I was sure she knew that I hadn't started to menstruate yet, and she was just showing off and trying to make me feel bad. And she succeeded—I felt completely left out, and it seemed as if everyone were growing up except me. And I was certain that when I finally did start, I would suddenly turn into an adult and I'd never feel so childishly self-conscious again.

But guess what? I was wrong! The day I actually got my period for the first time, I was so excited. Of course, I told my mom. And what did she do? She got on the phone and called up everybody we knew, and I could hear her saying, "Oh, you'll never believe it, but Jill finally got her period today, blah blah blah," and I just knew I'd never be able to look those people in the face again.

And then, as if that weren't mortifying enough, I found out that going to the supermarket to buy tampons or sanitary pads is possibly the most embarrassing thing in the world. You never pause in front of those shelves—you just look them over as fast as you can and snatch up what you need before anybody notices. And naturally there are always a couple of guys wandering slowly along that aisle just as you're picking out the box you want, so you have to turn around quickly and reach for the toothpaste! Then you hide the box under whatever else you've got in your cart, but when you get to the checkout counter, there's a guy instead of a girl ringing things up—probably some really cute guy you've seen around high school or your best friend's gorgeous older brother.

I'm sure you know exactly how it goes. What happens next? Either the machine doesn't work right and he has to yell across the store to find out the price of this particular item, or his buddy wanders in and leans on the end of the counter for a chat, or the register tape breaks, and you have to wait while the manager comes to fix it. But whatever it is that happens, it's always at the very moment when the guy is either ringing up your tampons or he's waving the box around in the air. And you just want to sink through the floor or run away. But you're stuck there—you can't very well leave while the rest of your stuff is being rung up!

I guess you can't win. There's always something to feel self-conscious about, no matter what stage of your life you're in. But luckily I found a solution to this particular problem—I made my mom buy all that stuff for me.

And she didn't mind—she's an old hand at it by now! Maybe when I'm her age, I won't feel embarrassed about it either!

MAKING CHOICES FOR AND ABOUT YOURSELF

While you're going through this time of figuring out who you are and who you're becoming, other people's opinions of you start to seem very important. It's as if you were bouncing reflections of yourself off their mirrors. If you do something totally outrageous, and all your friends say, "Hey, what's the matter with you?" it might tell you that you've gone a little too far in one direction. Or if you do something nice or if you help someone who's upset, everyone may give you a lot of approval and respect, and that makes you feel good about yourself. Trying to see yourself as other people see you can be a good method of testing the ways you're changing.

But it can be a little dangerous too. After all, you're the person who has to live with yourself, and in the long run you have to feel good about who you are no matter what anyone else thinks. Some girls find that when they go to a new school or when they enter junior high or high school, they start going around with a whole new group of kids. It's fun and exciting, but sometimes it turns out that this group is swept up in a bunch of stuff that you don't want to be involved in. They might be the kind who make fun of anyone who's serious about studying and getting good grades; or they might be into things you really don't approve of, like drugs or shoplifting; or they might just be a lot more ready for serious dating than you are.

It's hard to break out of a group like this once you've become one of the crowd. You cringe when you think of how they'll laugh at you or tell you you're weird. And nobody wants to be an outcast. But after a while you may find you don't feel very happy about them or about yourself. As you learn more about who you really are you can admit to yourself that this group isn't right for you, and you'll be able to move away from them.

When I was a junior in high school, a lot of kids I knew

started drinking. They thought it was really cool to get drunk and act kind of wild, but it never appealed to me much. I don't need to drink to have a good time, and I think it's kind of scary when kids come to school in the morning totally wiped out from drinking too much the night before. I even know one person who was an alcoholic by the age of eighteen, and I think that's really sad.

Fortunately, for most people I know, the drinking was just a phase they had to go through. Last New Year's Eve I went to a party, and no one had anything alcoholic to drink at all. I thought that was great because I didn't have to worry about any of them driving home. I'm a real worrier, and I've been at lots of parties where I've driven other kids home. I'd rather do that than wonder if they're going to make it home in one piece. But the strange thing is, it often seems as if the people who are drinking aren't even having much fun. It's as if they're just doing it because they think that's the way to be accepted.

Of course, it's not always this heavy. But teenagers often find they are trying to live up to what other people expect of them instead of working toward discovering their own identities. I can remember when I had started working on *The Love Boat* and I was still commuting to my old school in Livermore. I would walk down the hall and say hello to everybody, even kids I'd never been very friendly with. I was so afraid that if I didn't, they'd think I was conceited and stuck-up because of my job on TV. I really worried about it.

Now that seems kind of dumb to me. I've learned that I can't be good friends with everyone I happen to see walking down the street, and I also can't let total strangers dictate how I act. But at the time it seemed to me that I had to have everyone's approval and I'd fall apart if anyone thought anything bad about me. When I start feeling insecure now, I try to remember this experience. It seems that if you try to please the whole world, you never have time to be yourself—you just keep worrying all the time about what everyone is thinking.

I'm not suggesting that anyone should go around being mean and rude. There are people who are so full of themselves that they don't care if they hurt someone else's feelings. I can't stand that. One time my mom was at an antique show, and a very popular comedian was standing in front of her. My brother was a big fan of this man's, so Mom thought it would give my brother a thrill to have his autograph. Finally she got up the nerve to ask him to sign her program. He was really unpleasant about it, and even though he signed it, he made her feel terrible.

When she came home, she was still upset about it. She told me how rude he'd been and how humiliated she had felt. I don't think there's any excuse for that kind of behavior, especially from an entertainer, and I hope I never act that way.

DON'T THEY NOTICE THAT YOU'RE GROWING UP?

There's another way that other people's views of you can get in your way or make things a little difficult, and that's when they don't seem to realize that you're not a child anymore. I've found that people I've met since I was about sixteen treat me as more of a grown-up. But there are other people who I worked with several years ago, and they still act as if I were a little girl. Of course, part of my problem is that my character, Vicki Stubing, stayed quite young for a long time—younger than I was in real life. So a lot of people just think of me as being Vicki's age. It gets pretty annoying sometimes!

I'm lucky as far as my work is concerned, because on *The Love Boat* they change the stories so that the Vicki character can grow older. I'll still be playing the same part, but I won't be doing those cute little-girl things now—I'll be doing stories that are about an eighteen-year-old girl. I'm glad about that.

Sometimes it doesn't work out quite the way I hope it will. One time I was in Hong Kong doing one of our *Love Boat* specials. It was supposed to be my first big romantic scene, and I was really excited about it. We were up at the top of Victoria Peak, where there's a gorgeous view of the harbor and all the boats. But the problem was, it was pouring rain, and my hair was absolutely plastered to my face.

So I didn't look very romantic or glamorous. And the other problem was, the guy I was doing the love scene with was Leigh McCloskey from *Dallas*. He's a wonderful person and a fine actor, but I couldn't really feel too romantic about him. He's a good friend of mine—almost like a brother—and his wife is one of my best friends! So my big opportunity to have a grown-up love scene didn't change anybody's attitude about me, not even my own. But I figured, Better luck next time!

Lots of other child actors are in shows that just can't be changed as they get older—their character is always supposed to be eight or eleven or whatever. And when those actors get too old and grow out of the part, they have to leave the show. I'm glad *The Love Boat* isn't like that—it's fun for me to be growing up on the show and getting a chance to do different kinds of stories.

But sometimes in real life you can get stuck in a part that's too young for you. Maybe your grandmother still pinches your cheek and calls you her little dumpling and sends you a doll for Christmas. It's not so bad if it's just your grandmother who does this, and you only have to put up with it once a year. However, what if your parents don't give you any more freedom and responsibility than you had three years ago? That's hard to deal with.

People always say that you should just sit down and discuss this problem with your parents. You should, but sometimes it doesn't help very much. Parents who fail to notice that their little girl has become a teenager may not really hear you when you tell them. On the other hand it might be that a talk with them will open their eyes. It's definitely worth a try.

I guess it's hard for parents to let go of a child and to loosen the reins. After all, it means they're getting older themselves, and that might be something they don't like to think about. And you can understand that they worry about you and want to keep you safe, although that doesn't help much with the problem.

I remember when I was first starting to drive. I had taken all the classes and I'd passed my test. But my mom was really nervous about the whole idea, and she made a lot of rules about what I could do. Her rules were: no driving at night, no driving on the freeways, and no driving on the canyon roads.

Well, no driving at night wasn't so bad. But if you've ever been to Los Angeles, you know that you can't get much of anywhere without going on a freeway. And from my house you can't even get to a main street without going through one of the canyons between the San Fernando Valley and the city. So what it amounted to was that I couldn't drive more than about a block from home!

Even at the time I knew that she really trusted me—it was just that she was afraid of what can happen to anyone who drives a car. On the one hand she was glad that I could go places by myself and she didn't have to chauffeur me everywhere anymore. But on the other hand I think she was upset because it meant I wasn't going to be her little baby girl any longer. And after I'd been driving for a while and she saw that nothing terrible had happened, she got much more relaxed about the whole thing.

You may have a similar kind of problem—your parents aren't giving you enough freedom. The only advice I've ever heard that makes sense to me is to start *acting* more grown-up on your own. This means more than just talking about it. Even stuff like keeping your room cleaned up without being nagged about it or not staying out past your curfew shows them that you're able to handle more responsibility than before. It might take quite a while, and I'm not saying it's easy, but it may be the only way that works!

SO EMBARRASSED, YOU COULD DIE!

Before *The Love Boat* moved to our new studio in Hollywood, the show was filmed on the 20th Century Fox lot at the edge of Century City in West Los Angeles. It was an exciting place because someone was always shooting a feature film, and a lot of other TV shows were made there, like *M*A*S*H, Charlie's Angels, Dynasty, Family,* and *Starsky and Hutch.*

I loved going to work every day. The road to the main gate went right through the middle of the set for *Hello,*

Dolly!, so instead of going past boring office buildings, it was like driving along through this wonderful old city. I felt as if we'd been transported back in time to a whole different era of our country. If you saw the movie, you'll know the atmosphere I mean—it was a great way to start my working day!

Most days we ate lunch in the studio commissary, which is like a big restaurant for all the people who work on the lot. One time I was sitting at a table with my mom and I saw Paul Michael Glaser at another table across the room. I was really excited—I think he is wonderful! So I wrote a note to him and asked the waiter to take it to his table. What I meant to write was "I am your biggest fan," but what I actually said in the note was "Paul Michael Glaser, you are my biggest fan"!

It wasn't until the waiter was handing him the note that I realized what I'd written on that piece of paper. I couldn't believe it! I dived under the table in the middle of the restaurant and I wouldn't come out until he had left.

It had to be the most embarrassing moment of my life. I felt really stupid, and I thought if I ever saw him again on the lot, I'd just run away and hide. I wouldn't be able to face him. And I knew he must have thought I was a total idiot. I'd always wanted to meet him in person, but now I was sure that I'd never get the chance. Why would he want to be introduced to someone who sounded so conceited? I felt so bad. As Mom and I were leaving the commissary I ran over to the table he'd been sitting at and grabbed the linen napkin he had used. It was as close as I'd ever come to him! I think I still have that napkin put away somewhere.

As it turned out I did see Paul Michael Glaser soon after that on the lot, and he was so nice to me. He thought my mistake was kind of funny and cute, and he could understand how I'd been so excited that I got the words mixed up. From then on whenever he saw me, he'd say, "Oh, there's my little girlfriend," and put his arm around me.

I don't think there's a single person in the world who hasn't done something embarrassing like that. It happens all the time. The thing is, what seems completely terrible and stupid and embarrassing to you probably doesn't look that way at all to the other person. Either it's not important, and that person forgets about it thirty seconds after it happens—while you're going around for days blushing at the memory—or like Paul, the other person thinks it's a little bit funny or even endearing. Most people have had these embarrassing moments themselves, and they understand.

It's lucky that most people can be counted on to be understanding about this, because I'm still embarrassing myself all the time! When the Olympics were in Los Angeles, I went to the closing ceremonies with a girlfriend. We were sitting with a bunch of other people from ABC, and my friend and I were just going crazy—there were all these gorgeous athletes that had been in the Games and they were down on the field in front of us. These guys were so fabulous-looking, I thought I was about to die.

I guess my friend and I were making a lot of noise. And then I realized that Robert Guillaume (from *Benson*) was sitting right next to me! I felt terrible. I'm sure he thought we were a couple of screaming teenagers, and I knew I'd really made a fool of myself. It was definitely embarrassing! But later I decided that he probably understood that we were excited and just having a good time. After all, he was a teenager once himself!

WILL EVERYONE LAUGH AT ME?

When I was in grade school, I just hated it if anyone laughed at me. I wasn't very good in math, and one year I was in a math class that was really hard. A lot of times I just didn't understand what the teacher was explaining. But she had a rule that you couldn't go and ask her privately for help with the parts you didn't understand. You had to raise your hand in class and ask your questions then.

A couple of times I did raise my hand and ask a question. But there were some really smart kids in the class who always knew exactly what they were doing, and when I asked my dumb questions, they kind of snickered at me. Or at least I thought they did.

After that I just never raised my hand again. I couldn't stand the idea of other kids laughing at me and thinking I was so stupid. As a result I got further and further behind in class, and whenever we had a test, I'd want to stay home from school that day.

When I think about it now, I can see that it was silly to act that way. If I had had the nerve to ask my questions no matter what, maybe I would have understood what the class was all about and I wouldn't have felt so dumb the whole year. And guess what? I wasn't the only one who didn't follow what was going on in math. It turned out that other kids in the class were having trouble too. But they were just as afraid to look ignorant as I was.

It is hard to take the risk of having people laugh at you, and at that point in my life I guess I just couldn't do it. And even now I have a little trouble with it sometimes. I was having a birthday party at my house and I was really looking forward to it. But the day of the party I got the worst stomachache of my life! I just kept on worrying—what if no one came to the party? And if they did come, what if they didn't have a good time?

It was silly. The people I'd invited were my friends, so of course, they would come to my birthday party and have a good time! But I couldn't stop myself from feeling nervous and even a little scared about it. Still, the good part was that I didn't call off the party, and everyone came and had a lot of fun! I guess I've learned something about dealing with these feelings.

Sometimes we just have to steel ourselves and take a chance. And often it turns out that it wasn't such a big risk after all, and everything works out fine. Knowing that doesn't keep us from having a fluttery feeling in the pit of our stomachs, and maybe we'll never get over that entirely. My mom has given hundreds of parties, but she still gets nervous before each one! Still, for me it's a lot better than it used to be, and every time I make myself do something I'm nervous about, it gets a little easier.

FIRST YOU'RE UP, THEN YOU'RE DOWN

Everyone says that the early teen years are a time of emotional swings. You may be wildly happy one minute and then suddenly—for no reason you can think of—you're really depressed. It's kind of scary, because you feel as if you can't control your moods, and you don't know what you can do about them.

People have lots of theories about why this happens. One possible explanation is that until now you haven't really tried to control your emotions. When little kids get mad, they might scream or have a temper tantrum or even hit someone. And when they feel sad, they just burst into tears.

But as you become a teenager you start to feel that you can't really act this way anymore. You'd look pretty ridiculous if you threw yourself on the floor in a screaming fit every time your sister made you mad. The problem is, though, that being in control of your feelings is something you haven't done much before, and you have to learn how to do it. It shouldn't be too surprising that you can't control your moods very well at the moment.

Another possible reason for these crazy mood swings is that teenagers are going through a lot of physical changes. As you enter puberty your body begins to develop, and you start looking more like a woman and less like a child. At the same time all kinds of hormones are being activated, and it takes a while for them to settle down and be regulated the way they're supposed to. It seems likely that these drastic physical developments can have an effect on your emotions.

Did you ever think that what you eat might have something to do with how you feel? A lot of experts believe that nutrition plays an important part in balancing or unbalancing your emotions. Lots of teenagers have pretty strange eating habits from time to time. If you go through a phase of eating nothing but junk food, it may very well do some weird things to your emotions. And if you're dieting hard, you may not be getting enough food that's really nutritious, and that may be doing things you don't even know about to your psychological self.

Anyway, whatever it is that causes them, these up-and-down feelings are real, and you can't wish them away. The good news is that they won't last forever; most experts say that by the time you're sixteen, you'll be over this stage. But if this is happening to you now, it can be very confusing.

When you're feeling down, it's hard to make yourself do anything to feel better, even if you can think of something that would help. In fact, it's hard to make yourself do anything at all. Fortunately you do have to go to school. At least that makes you drag yourself out of bed and get out of the house every day.

I had to go to work as well as school, so I rarely got a chance to bury myself under the covers and give in to my emotions. A lot of times I wanted to! But I don't think it really helps to do that. If you drop out of your normal life and shut yourself away from other people, it just drags you deeper into your unhappiness.

You've probably heard something like this a million times. How often has your mother said to you, "Just get busy and do something, and it will put your problems into perspective"? Sometimes it sounds impossible to do. But it's worth a try. I think it works for me, and you might find that your blue mood lifts a little. And the worst that can happen is that you'll get some of the things done that you've been meaning to do.

Another bonus of getting yourself out in the world is that often someone says something to you unexpectedly that really helps. Once when I was feeling kind of depressed for some reason, I had to go back into the studio to get a book I'd left there. I asked one of the guards if he would unlock the room for me, and he said, "Sure, I'm always happy to do anything I can for you." I was surprised because I didn't know why he would do anything for me that he wouldn't do for anyone else. I guess he noticed that I looked startled. He reminded me that soon after I'd started working on the show, his granddaughter had been in the hospital. He'd asked all the cast members to sign a card for her, since she always watched *The Love Boat*. And I felt so sorry for her being in the hospital that I told him I'd call her up and tell her I hoped she got better soon. Apparently she was really thrilled that I called her, and she told everyone on the ward. She felt I'd done something special for her.

When he talked about it, it made me feel good. Obviously it had meant a lot to his granddaughter and to him, and they both still remembered it. It made me think I must be a pretty good person after all! The thing is, he didn't know I had been down in the dumps and he wasn't especially trying to cheer me up. But an incident like this can change your whole outlook just when you least expect it and need it most.

RUNAWAY EMOTIONS

When you're a teenager, little things frequently get blown way out of proportion. If you do poorly on a pop quiz in French, it can make you feel you're a complete failure. Or if you get up your courage to say hello to the gorgeous guy whose locker is next to yours, and he doesn't even answer you, you're ready to leave town and never show your face in that school again. And when you sit on a piece of chewing gum and someone makes a joke about it in front of the whole class, you may want to hide in the ladies' room and never come out.

It's pretty tough to keep things in perspective when your feelings are running away with you. Even though you know in one part of your mind that it was only a minor incident, you often can't help acting as if it were a major disaster. You blush, your hands feel clammy, sweat breaks out on your forehead, your heart starts pounding, and there doesn't seem to be anything you can do about it. It's awful!

I remember once when I was twelve or thirteen, I was doing a scene in the show and I blew my lines. That had hardly ever happened to me before, but it really was no big thing. I knew other people flubbed or forgot lines all the time, and no one ever got upset about it. The director would just call for a retake, and we'd do it over.

But I wasn't used to it for myself. I try really hard to learn my lines the night before, and I don't make those mistakes very often. So I got flustered. Then we started the scene over, and I messed up my lines again. By the third take I was totally out of control. I was crying and trembling all over, and I just couldn't get it right no matter how much I tried.

Everyone was very surprised at how I was reacting. Redoing scenes was a common occurrence, and nothing to get so upset about. I knew that myself, but I couldn't seem to stop making things worse and worse.

Finally the assistant director suggested that the cast and crew move on to shoot another scene. He was very kind and said they could come back and do my scene later. It was nice of him to offer me a way of getting out of the situation. But his saying that somehow made me realize that I didn't want to let this craziness get the best of me.

I told him, "No, I'll get it right the next time, I promise." We took a short break, and I used that time to calm down and think over what was happening. I didn't want to be unprofessional and make them spend a lot of time and money to change the shooting schedule just because I'd gotten hysterical. It wasn't easy to think about it rationally when I was still so unglued, but after a while I realized that the first time I'd goofed had really shaken me. It was so unexpected that I panicked. Instead of stopping to get hold of myself, I plunged on and made even more mistakes, and after that there was no way to stop the downward spiral.

Finally I blew my nose and put cold water on my eyes—I didn't want them to look all red and puffy. As the makeup man was fixing my face I decided that I would just start the scene as if that whole mess hadn't even happened. And sure enough, it went fine.

My mom said later that it was just my hormones acting up, and she was probably right. But it was horrible. I didn't like feeling that I didn't have any control over what I was doing. And I'm glad I'm past those early teen years when things like that happen to everyone!

It helped a little to know that it wasn't my fault. I really couldn't do anything about the changes my body was going through. And it helped a lot to realize that I did manage to calm down and go on. I felt good that I hadn't let my runaway emotions get the best of me.

ARE YOU WEARING A MASK?

As you might have already guessed, I'm the kind of person who likes to look on the bright side of things and keep my bad feelings locked away. I guess I'm a closet crier—I never like to let anyone see me upset, so I keep everything inside.

Maybe a lot of other teenagers are like this too. I don't know what you do when you get angry or sad or fed up with the world, but I often talk to my dogs. Sally and Melanie are tiny, fluffy, and really cute. They're a special breed called a Maltese poodle. Sally is all white, and she was the first one I got. When I played the lead in my high school production of *The Wizard of Oz*, I didn't get a bunch of roses at the end of the show on opening night as most leading ladies do. I got Sally instead! I was very excited, and she's been the greatest dog. I was really happy that my mom gave her to me.

Later on I was in a production of *Oklahoma!* at a community theater. Mom had bought Sally from some people who breed this kind of dog, and they came to see the show. And they gave me Melanie after that performance. She's black and white—and full of mischief. I really love both of them.

The great thing about dogs is that they're always there for you. They never criticize or ask questions and they're never too busy to play or just curl up in your lap for a cuddle. Sometimes I talk to them about whatever is bothering me. They're always interested, even though they don't have much advice for me! But just being around them often makes me feel better.

There are lots of people—like my mom and my friends—I can talk to about everything. But sometimes I just want to pour out my feelings without having anyone asking me questions or giving me suggestions about what to do. When I'm in that mood, I don't want to know what anyone else thinks. And dogs are great for that!

Sometimes I'm not really sure how I feel or what I'm upset about. Just talking out loud often helps me figure out what the problem is. But it's usually pretty confused, and it's not something I'd feel comfortable discussing with a real person.

At other times I really know underneath that whatever I'm upset about is pretty silly. It's nice to be able to say all kinds of weird things and not have the other person think you're nuts. Sally and Melanie don't have any idea if what I say makes sense. They'll just give me a lick or two because they can tell I'm not feeling too happy.

I don't think it's bad to keep some of your feelings to yourself. It's not always the right time or place to let everything out. But it's important to find some way to express your emotions, even if they're not all happy ones. Keeping everything bottled up can make you feel ready to explode. And it seems that these feelings always come out in some way—often not the way that would be the most helpful. For instance, you might end up having a huge screaming fight with your best friend when you're really mad at your mom about something, but you think you can't tell her about it. This just makes things worse.

You probably have a safety valve of your own—some way you can let off steam without hurting anyone's feelings. Sometimes if I'm mad at the world, I just go for a drive all by myself. Just concentrating on the curves in the mountain roads seems to put things in perspective. Maybe you put on your sweats and run around the track five times. Or you might write down your feelings in a diary that no one else is allowed to see.

Some people talk to their teddy bears just the way I talk to my dogs. When I was in elementary school, I had a Barbie doll and I talked to her a lot. Then one semester I changed schools—I started going to a private school instead of the public school I'd been attending. But I really didn't like it, and I got upset because the teachers used to hit the kids with a metal ruler when they acted up. So after half a year I went back to my old school. You'd think that would have been easy, but it seemed different and scary to me, and I was really nervous. So I took my Barbie doll to school with me the first day. She made me feel better and not so scared. The teacher could see how I was clutching the doll, I guess, and she let me keep her at my desk the whole day.

But it's not always enough to have your private way of expressing your angry or unhappy feelings. There are times when it's really better to talk to the person you have a problem with. After all, if you don't tell them what's going on and what you're thinking, how will they ever find out? And how will they ever change their behavior if they don't know they're doing something that's bothering you?

I know it's the right thing to do, but I'm not very good at confronting people this way. When I was on my diet, I was being really strict about what I ate. The only snack I could have all day was an apple—but I got to eat the whole thing. And I'm really picky about what kind of apples I get! What I'd do is cut it into the skinniest slices I could make so it would take longer to eat. Then I had this little dish of cinnamon and sugar substitute mixed together. I'd dip each slice into the cinnamon mixture and then eat it real slowly.

One day I was on the set, and I had some time before the next scene. So I got my apple all sliced up and ready. But as soon as I started eating it someone came over and said, "Oh, that looks great. Can I have a slice?"

I didn't want to give it to him—it was the only thing I'd be able to eat until dinner! But I didn't know how to say no. So I just shrugged and didn't say anything at all, and a couple of slices disappeared into his mouth.

Five minutes later someone else came over, and the same thing happened again. I was gritting my teeth, and by the time the third person grabbed a couple of apple slices, I was ready to scream. But I didn't.

What I should have said was "I'm sorry, but this is part of my diet and I have to eat all of it." That wouldn't have been rude, and it would have stopped people from taking a little slice here and there all the time. And it would have kept me from feeling so angry at them.

In a way this is a pretty silly story, but it shows what I mean. Everybody shares food on the set all the time, and the people who came over had no way of knowing that my apple was different. Furthermore, they're my friends—it shouldn't have been so hard to explain to them how I felt. But I was annoyed, and I felt I couldn't let them know that. The next time some little problem like this comes up, I hope I can remember this incident and learn to say what's on my mind. Keeping it to myself just made me brood over it for much too long. And that's really dumb—especially when a few words could have prevented the whole thing.

FOLLOW YOUR STAR!

I knew from the time I was a little girl that I wanted to be an actress. Most people don't know so early what they want to do with their lives, but I did, and I worked really hard to make it happen. Being on a TV series isn't all glamor—there's a lot of hard work involved. But I won't pretend I didn't enjoy the glamor part of it too! I loved meeting the really famous people who were guest stars on the show. It may sound kind of corny, but I always asked them for an autographed picture and I have a whole wall in my house filled with photos of my idols who've been on *The Love Boat*, like Lana Turner, Olivia De Havilland, Ginger Rogers, Ethel Merman, Debbie Reynolds, Juliet Prowse, and Linda Evans.

I remember when Lana Turner was a guest star on one of the *Love Boat* cruises. I was thrilled—I think she's such a wonderful actress. So at one point I went up to her and said how terrific I thought she was and how I really admired her. And she said to me, "You know, I've watched you since you started on the show, and it's such an honor to meet you."

It totally floored me! I was thinking, *No*, I just couldn't believe she had said that to me, and she even said it right in front of our producer.

As you can imagine, I was on cloud nine for the rest of the day. And when I thought about it later, I was even happier, because what she said made me realize that I had begun to accomplish some of the goals I had set for myself, and I was becoming successful at what I wanted to do.

Of course, that doesn't mean it will last. A lot of people are successful for a while in TV or the movies, and then for some unknown reason they aren't anymore. I know of someone who was on a TV series for quite a while, but she hasn't worked much lately, and not long ago I saw her as an extra in a movie. That's kind of sad, and I don't want that to happen to me. I don't think I'd let it happen. I want to be the best at what I do, and if I couldn't be the best as an actress, then I'd find something else that I could be really good at. Does that sound too ambitious or conceited? I hope not. I think of it as having respect for myself and believing in myself and the career I've chosen.

GROWING UP AT YOUR OWN PACE

Being a teenager really is being in between. We're not kids and we're not adults. And although we're moving toward adulthood, at times it seems we're going very, very slowly—even backward. And then, maybe the very next day, we shoot forward and feel all grown-up—childhood seems so far behind us.

This can be pretty confusing, not only to us but to everyone around us. People tell me that one day I act like a little kid and then the next day I act like a grown-up woman. They probably don't know who they're talking to from one minute to the next!

I know they're right. I do feel like a child sometimes and like an adult at other times. And it gets annoying when I'm feeling really together—as if I know what I'm doing and where I'm going—that's the time people treat me like a ten-year-old. Or the other way around—I might feel as though I don't want to deal with grown-up stuff right at the moment, and then someone expects me to act like I'm thirty!

I guess it just takes time to get this age problem in sync, both for myself and for the people around me. But I do feel a lot older and wiser than I used to. Sometimes I look back at my grade-school years and I think, *If only I knew then what I know now!* Everything would have been so much easier.

Of course, that isn't really true. What I know now is what makes sense for someone my age, not for the younger girl I was then. A lot of times in grade school or junior high when I was upset or unhappy about something, I'd tell my mom about it. She always had some ideas about what I should say or do to make things better. But it was strange. A couple of times I tried doing exactly what she'd suggested, and the other kids looked at me as if I were from outer space. They just couldn't relate to whatever it was I'd said. It might have been that I repeated the exact words my mom had used, and it really didn't sound like "kid talk." But I think the problem was that she was using adult logic to solve the situation, and it just didn't work for me and my friends.

Maybe what I'm trying to say is that it's better to act in a way that's appropriate for your age. You might wonder what's wrong with a teenager who still chooses to wear frilly little-girl clothes and likes to play with the toys she had in third grade. But it works the other way too. I'm sure you've seen thirteen-year-old girls who are trying to look twenty-one. They may be well-developed physically and they may wear slinky, sexy clothes and lots of makeup. It's kind of sad, because most people end up thinking that these girls just look silly and kind of pathetic.

A while back there was a girl who did a guest spot on *The Love Boat*. She was only about a year older than me, but you would never have guessed it—she was real sexy, and she looked as if she were in her early twenties.

I went out to lunch with her, and I must have been complaining about my character on the show staying so young. This actress said very seriously, "Jill, you've got to change your image. Why don't you have some artistic nude photos taken? Then you could get them published in one of those men's magazines."

I was kind of shocked. I mean, I wanted Vicki to grow up a little, but appearing as a centerfold in a men's magazine wasn't the way I wanted to do it! I'm sure this actress really meant to be helpful, but obviously we were coming from totally different places.

It isn't always easy to know what *is* right for your age, because you feel both grown-up and childlike at the same time. But often if you take time to think through what you're doing, you find out what feels right for you. Each person grows up at her own pace. There are lots of things people tell you "for your own good," and most of the time they're probably right. It's perfectly good advice. But even if they are right, if you're not ready to see things that way, it's not going to work.

If you've been a regular viewer of *The Love Boat*, you probably noticed that there was a time when I got kind of chubby. Actually it was worse than that—I got fat! It kind of crept up on me, and for a while no one said anything about it. But there came a point when everybody decided I ought to do something about it. My mom got on my case, the directors of the show suggested that I'd look better on film if I were thinner, and my friends on the set started making pointed remarks.

I knew they were right. I could see how I looked in the mirror, and I couldn't help noticing that my clothes didn't fit anymore. But it took another few months before I got myself together and went on my diet. I don't think it was just because I'm stubborn—although I am! I think I just wasn't ready to decide for myself that I had to do it.

Knowing when you're ready for something in your life isn't always easy. And saying you're not ready can be a convenient excuse for not doing what you know you should do. But if you can be honest with yourself and listen to your own signals, it makes things go a lot more smoothly. I think this is one of the most important things you can learn as a teenager. It's a way of finding out who you really are and of being true to the real you.

Here, and at the end of every chapter in this book, I have included some letters I've received from other teenage girls, wanting to share their experiences with me or wanting to know how I handle certain situations. I always try to answer each letter as honestly and as wisely as I can.

Dear Jill,

I'm so shy, I can hardly do anything. I have trouble trying to talk to other girls, and as for boys, forget it! If a teacher calls on me in class, I blush and stammer, even though I know the answer.

I feel like I'll never have any social life at all if I can't get over this. Is there anything I can do about my problem?

Deby M.

Dear Deby,

If on the inside you're not as shy as you appear on the outside, being shy can make it harder for you to get places you want to go in your life. A lot of my friends had this problem, and many of them found that taking speech classes or joining the debating club or drama group at school was a great way to start overcoming it.

Maybe you've heard this advice before and it sounded scary so you didn't try it. But trust me, it works! When you know you have to talk in front of a teacher who's grading you, it makes you forget about the other kids listening. And when you're acting on stage, there's nothing to feel shy or nervous about because it isn't really you saying those lines, it's the character you're playing. I think this kind of experience can help you get over some of your shyness, and besides, it's a great way to meet a lot of interesting people.

Dear Jill,

I don't know what's the matter with me, but everything in my life seems to be going wrong lately. I'm doing poorly in two of my classes at school, and I'm afraid I might fail them. And my mom seems to be always yelling at me about something, such as my room is a mess or she doesn't like my haircut. I had a big fight with my best friend—she's not talking to me, and I'm really upset. I just don't know what to do. How can I get my life together again?

Melissa R.

Dear Melissa,

I know how you feel. Sometimes it does seem as if everything goes wrong all at the same time. But you can take action to make things better.

First get your priorities straight. What's your biggest problem at the moment? I'd say it's your schoolwork, and that's what you should do something about right away. Try to analyze the situation. Is the work too hard so you can't keep up because you don't understand it? If so, you can get help. Ask your teacher for extra time, or get a friend or tutor to work with until you get caught up. On the other hand your problem may be that you just aren't studying. If so, that's something only you can change. Set aside time each night to do your work, and don't let anything interfere with it. Once you get into the habit, it's not so hard, and you'll feel good after you do it. I know that for myself.

As for keeping your room neat, I have the same problem, so I know what you mean! Try putting everything away as soon as you use it—put your clothes right into the hamper when you take them off or right back on the hanger in the closet. That way you won't ever have to say, "Okay, Saturday is Clean-Up-My-Room Day!" This method takes only two seconds if you keep at it.

Once you start working on these two problems, I think you'll find that your mom will get off your case. She's probably most worried about your schoolwork, and when she sees that you're trying to keep your room straightened up, she's likely to ease up on other things, and the two of you can get back to better communication. You might want to ask her to help you make time for studying—I'm sure she'll try to keep the distractions to a minimum when she knows you're really trying.

In fact, I believe that when you've got a plan in operation for solving your most important problems, you'll come out of your tailspin. Right now you can't help taking out your frustration on everyone around you, and that probably had a lot to do with the fight with your friend. She'll probably get over being mad at you very soon, and if she doesn't, you'll be in better shape to discuss it with her when things are going better for you in other areas.

Good luck! I know you can do it!

Dear Jill,

All of a sudden it seems that the girls I hang around with do nothing but talk about boys. They're always gossiping about who likes who and how they can get boys to ask them out. Talking about boys that way makes me nervous, but I feel left out when I'm with my friends. Is there something wrong with me?

Susan B.

Dear Susan,

I'm sure there's nothing wrong with you at all. It sounds to me as if you just aren't ready yet for boy-girl relationships and dating, and that's perfectly okay. There's nothing worse than going on a date because everyone says you should if you don't really feel comfortable doing it. It's much better to wait until you're ready for it, and don't worry—that time will come!

In the meantime, though, you don't really have to tell all your girlfriends how you feel. You may be concerned that they'll think you're weird or babyish, and I don't think there's any need to put yourself in a position where they'll make fun of you. Maybe you can just listen and sort of look interested—you might pick up some tips about boys for later! And it doesn't matter that you aren't actually going out on dates. Plenty of girls talk about boys a lot even though they're hardly dating at all.

The main thing is that there's nothing wrong with you. We all mature at different speeds, and by next year I bet you'll be as "boy-crazy" as anybody else!

Chapter 2

Life Aboard *The Love Boat*

LOTS OF PEOPLE ask me what it was like "growing up" on television. I guess it sounds like a really glamorous life, full of parties, travel, and chances to meet famous stars. That's partly true, and I'm certainly not complaining. Because the show I'm on takes place on a cruise ship, I get to go to lots of exciting countries. Most of the time we're shooting in the studio in Hollywood, but every year we go away for about six weeks to a different part of the world. For example, we've been to the Far East (including China!), to Europe and the Soviet Union, to the Mediterranean countries and Israel, to Australia and Fiji, and of course, to the Caribbean and Mexico.

If it weren't for the show, I would never have gotten the chance to see all these fabulous places. That's one of the things I've appreciated most about being a regular character on *The Love Boat*. It was so exciting to see with my own eyes the famous sights and the countries I'd studied in social studies classes. One of the neatest things that happened was in Australia. When I had some time off, we went to a park where there were lots of koala bears. They were so cute, just like cuddly stuffed animals, and one of the little ones ran up my leg! I couldn't believe I got to hold a real koala! In fact, I was so excited about it that, before we left Australia, I made my mom drive me back to the park, which was forty-five minutes away, so I could say good-bye to my little friend.

I take lots of pictures everywhere, and I have a whole collection of photo albums that I love to look through. In Japan I took a whole bunch of pictures of the beautiful temples and people at the Tokyo Disneyland. One of my favorite pictures is one where I'm all dressed up in a formal kimono. You wouldn't believe how long it takes to put one on! First you get wrapped up in a kind of cloth binding—it's really tight, and it's hard to move in it. Then there's a thin under-kimono and after that the fancy brocade kimono itself, and both of them have to be arranged just right. And then they put on the obi sash. On my feet I had the special one-toed socks and the fancy white sandals.

This formal costume is what ladies wear to perform the tea ceremony, and the people who dressed me really had to know what they were doing! I got made up to look Japanese, and I wore a wig with the long hairpins that are used with the ceremonial costume. What was really amazing was that while I was standing outside having my picture taken in the costume, some Japanese people came up and started talking to me in Japanese! Those wardrobe and makeup people sure were good at their jobs!

I really splurged to buy that kimono and bring it home with me because I thought it was so gorgeous. Usually I try to buy some fairly big item in each country I visit, and it's always something that's special to that place. For instance, they make fabulous leather clothing in Turkey, and it's a lot less expensive than it would be here in the United States. And the best part is that you can show them a picture of what you want, and they'll make it for you. So when I was there, I got some leather pants and a couple of really nice jackets.

Of course, it's fun to buy gifts for my friends and family that are special reminders of each country. Last time we were in the Caribbean, I bought some perfume for my grandmother. She really loves perfume, and in Curaçao I could buy her favorite kind for almost nothing. And at the same time I got a little crystal turtle for my friend who has a turtle collection. In Japan the thing to buy is photographic and stereo equipment, so when we were there, I got some special lenses for my dad, and I also got a neat little stereo for myself. Actually I got one for my best friend too—it was such a great deal that I couldn't help going a little overboard! All my friends seem to love T-shirts from other countries, so I try to find some interesting ones, like the ones I brought back from the Tokyo Disneyland.

GOING ON A *LOVE BOAT* CRUISE

When our show goes on one of the cruises, it's not just a matter of packing our suitcases and taking off. For one thing, there must be about a hundred people altogether, including the cast and the crew.

And the ship is always a regular cruise ship—it's not one that's used only for filming our show. That means we have to take along a huge amount of equipment—everything from cameras and lights to makeup and wardrobe. We have a great crew, and they work very hard on these cruises.

Parts of the show are filmed on land in the different ports we're going to. At each stop the crew has to haul all the equipment off the boat to wherever we're going to be shooting, and then at the end of the day they have to haul it all back onto the boat again. This is because a cruise ship usually stops at each port for one day only, and then at night the ship travels to the next port. Sometimes the ship can stop for only half a day, and then everybody really has to hustle to get finished in time.

Of course, we film on board the ship, too, and that's kind of like shooting at the studio. But when the workday is over, we're all still there together on the boat. Then we get to join in the regular cruise activities with the other passengers.

The *Love Boat* cruises are real cruises, and there are lots of passengers who aren't connected with the show. Some of them like to come and watch when we're shooting scenes, and sometimes they're in the shots of the pool or the deck. We've gotten to know some people pretty well over the years because they make plans to go on the *Love Boat* cruise for their vacation every year. It's fun when we see our old friends again, and when I'm not in a scene or I have a break, I may go and play Bingo with them or sit and talk while I'm soaking up some sun.

But when I'm on our *Love Boat* cruises, I'm not simply relaxing and having a good time like the regular passengers. We're filming segments of the show, and I'm working. There are lots of times when I'd like to lie on deck beside the pool or hang out with people I've met on the boat, but if my scenes are being filmed, I've got to know my lines and be prepared to do a run-through. Even though filming a show always involves a lot of waiting around, I can't just go off and do what I want to do. I have to stay near the set and be ready for whenever I'm needed.

Since the *Love Boat* has to keep to its cruise schedule, we have to arrange our filming around it. The cruises are usually in May or June, and I remember when we were in Stockholm, I had arranged to leave the ship there and fly home for my high school graduation, which was the next day. My last scene was to take place on board the ship, and we were shooting it in port so that I could go and catch my plane when it was over. But it was one of those days when everything got delayed. The boat had to leave when it was scheduled to leave, and I was terrified that we wouldn't finish the scene in time. If we hadn't, I would have had to stay on the ship to film it the next day, and I would have missed my graduation!

The ship's engines were warming up, and its crew was almost ready to pull up the gangplank when the director finally said, "Okay, that's a wrap!" I ran as fast as I could, pulling off my cruise costume and throwing on my own clothes while everybody was yelling, "Happy graduation!" I didn't really believe I was going to make it until the plane took off for Los Angeles!

It's sort of complicated to explain, but in addition to filming scenes on the cruise ship and in the ports where it makes short stops, we shoot parts of the shows in other cities while we're away. We might go to London or Paris and stay in a hotel for a few days or even a week. I love doing that because usually I have enough time off to see the city. On my first trip to Paris I was really excited because there were so many things I wanted to do. We had only three days there, and I had a lot of scenes to shoot, but my schedule gave me quite a bit of free time. At least it did on paper. But something got held up somewhere, and I ended up hanging around in the hotel lobby for one entire day waiting for the van to pick me up—and it never came! I couldn't even jump into a taxi and take a quick ride to the Eiffel Tower because I was on call, and no one knew when they would need me. I guess I'll have to go back to Paris and see the things I missed.

One of the best parts of taking these trips is the chance to meet people who live in other countries. We've been invited into their homes and we've really gotten to see how they live. It's often very different from life in the United States, but I've discovered that people are basically the same everywhere. They've always been warm and friendly and welcoming.

Sometimes I've gotten to meet some pretty famous people as well. In Monaco we were shooting a scene outside the royal palace, and all of a sudden we realized that Prince Albert had come out to say hello. He was just wearing a polo shirt and jeans and at first nobody recognized him! And when we were in England, I almost had dinner with Prince Andrew. But at the last minute he had to go away to do some kind of military service. I was so disappointed!

HOW I GOT STARTED IN ACTING

It seems that ever since I was a little girl, I've known I wanted to be an actress. When I was little, I acted in several shows at community theaters in northern California, and I loved doing it. The first time I got on stage in front of an audience, I knew this was what I truly wanted, and after that I pestered my mom to take me to auditions for anything that was going on. Then some of my friends were planning to enter the California Little Miss pageant, so I decided I wanted to do it too. The real reason I wanted to be in it was because I wanted a crown!

The California Little Miss pageant was run by the same people who run the Miss America pageant, and it was a lot of fun. Every girl got a trophy for something, so even if you weren't the winner, you didn't feel bad. I remember that the night before, my dad read me the rules of the competition and one of them was that you had to be nice to the other girls. So when they were announcing the winners, I was standing on stage holding hands with a girl I'd made friends with there! They started out with the fourth runner-up and then the third runner-up, just like they do in the Miss America pageant. And when the announcer said, "And this year's California Little Miss is . . . Jill Whelan!," I couldn't believe it! I've still got my crown!

I was taking acting classes in San Francisco, and figured out that if I wanted to be on TV, I would have to have an agent. So when I was eight, I sent the pictures of me that I liked best to an agent whose name I had found out on my own. I guess it was the right thing to do, because after that I was in some commercials, including a national one for M&M's candy.

When I got a lead role in a new TV series, I was thrilled, and I was sure it was my big break. But the show, called *Friends*, lasted only a few episodes and of course, I felt crushed when it was cancelled. As it turned out, doing *Friends* really *was* my big break after all, because that's how I met the producer Aaron Spelling. He's also one of the executive producers of *The Love Boat*, and I did a guest appearance on that show.

Apparently they got a lot of letters from people who

had liked me in the show; they asked if they would be seeing more of Captain Stubing's daughter, Vicki. So there I was in Livermore, feeling depressed because *Friends* had been canceled, when all of a sudden Aaron Spelling called. At first I didn't believe it was him; I couldn't believe an important man like Mr. Spelling would ever take the time to call me. He said, ''Jill, how would you like to be a regular on *The Love Boat*?'' And of course, I just went crazy!

MY *LOVE BOAT* "FAMILY"

The people on the show really are like members of my family. Part of the reason I feel that way is because I was very young when I started on the show, and I've grown up with the cast and crew. It's great because we spend so much time together, what with our six weeks of travel every year and all the time we spend on the set. The regulars, like Gavin MacLeod, Bernie Kopell, Fred Grandy, and Ted Lange, are in practically every episode, and they work every week the show is filming, even though how much you see of them in the final show varies according to that week's story.

On *The Love Boat* I play the part of Vicki Stubing, Captain Stubing's daughter, and Gavin MacLeod has played the Captain since the show started. Gavin is really a neat person, and I love and admire him a lot. He and the rest of the regulars are always very supportive and helpful. I remember when I started on the show, everybody was very nice to me. On my very first day the producers came by and said they wanted to welcome me to *The Love Boat*, and they stayed to watch for almost the whole day. And when I was at the coffee machine getting some cream of chicken soup (that's what I always had), Lauren Tewes, who played Julie then, came up and said how nice it was to have me in the cast. That same day Gavin gave me a little necklace that said *I Love You*. You can imagine that it all made me feel really welcome.

INSIDE THE STUDIO

The Love Boat is filmed, not taped. Television shows that are recorded on videotape, like most sitcoms, have a different kind of weekly schedule from ours. They're done more like plays. During the first part of the week the cast rehearses the show. Then when it's taped, the scenes are done in order from beginning to end.

But film isn't done the same way. Doing our show is a lot like making a short movie every week. The scenes are not shot in order; in fact, the welcome-aboard scene could be shot at the end of the week after the rest of the story is done. It doesn't matter because the final show is spliced together from these individual shots by the film editor.

When I'm in Los Angeles, my day usually begins early and ends late. Now that I've turned eighteen and am no longer a minor, I am allowed by law to work much longer hours than before. Often I'm expected to be on the set by six-thirty in the morning and I don't get finished until almost eight at night. But even before this year, when I was still in high school, I had long days.

They weren't allowed to call me to the set until seven-thirty in the morning, but I still had to get up, take a shower, wash my hair, and be ready for my mom to drive me to the studio. Some mornings it was really hard—I just didn't feel like climbing out of bed and getting myself put together.

When I got there at seven-thirty, my first stop was the makeup room. Luckily our show has the most wonderful makeup man. Bob has been on the show a long time. He would always greet me with a grin and give me a cheery "Good morning, Jill." Even when I was still half asleep or felt real grumpy, I couldn't help smiling back at him.

My hair has always been pretty easy to take care of, and I wash it myself every morning, so my stop at the hairdressers' section wasn't very long. They have to do the hairstyling for everyone on the show and are usually pretty busy setting hot rollers and things like that so I would sometimes just borrow the blow dryer and do the little bit that needed to be done myself.

Since *The Love Boat* is a cruise show, everyone who works on the ship is supposed to be fairly tan. If I'm not tan enough myself, I have to get body makeup on my arms and legs. Margie is the body-makeup lady, and she's become a surrogate mother and good friend over the years. She's older than me, but I feel she's someone I can confide in, so we always have lots to say to each other while she's putting on my body makeup. I prefer not to have body makeup because it rubs off on my regular clothes and then I've got to get them washed or dry-cleaned, but sometimes I need it.

Like all shows, *The Love Boat* provides wardrobe for all the actors and actresses who appear in the weekly segments. Joie is the wardrobe mistress for *The Love Boat*, and she shops in regular stores for all our outfits that aren't uniforms. She knows everybody's size, and it's up to her to pick out things that will look right for the part each character plays. Sometimes she doesn't have to buy things. The studio has a big wardrobe department full of clothes of different kinds that have been used on various shows, such as *Dynasty* and *Matt Houston*. Often there's something that will work fine for one of our episodes. And of course our ship uniforms are made especially for us.

There is also a wardrobe person who is on the set every minute we're working. Her name is Frances, and she has to make sure everything looks right before the camera starts rolling. It's amazing to see the clever tricks she uses sometimes! For instance, there's this stuff called toupé tape. It's clear double-faced tape that men can use to anchor their toupés to their bald heads! But on the set Frances uses it to fix our clothes. She might stick down the end of a belt that keeps flapping or use it to anchor something like slipping shoulder pads or a hem that's ripped. Another problem toupé tape can solve is a lowcut dress that gapes open too much when an actress leans over—that doesn't look good on TV!

Whenever I have time, I go shopping with Joie for the clothes I'll be wearing on upcoming shows. I love shopping, and naturally I try to talk her into going to some of the expensive boutiques in Los Angeles. I can't afford to buy clothes for myself in these places, but it's great to try their things on! And every now and then Joie gives in and gets me something terrific for the show.

Up until recently my character, Vicki, was supposed to be quite young. That was fine when I first started on the show, but when I turned fifteen, it started to get to me. Boy, did I get tired of all those little-girl puff sleeves and princess dresses—and most of all, the Mary Jane shoes! Of course, I understood why they dressed me like that, but I felt pretty dumb, especially when there was a cute guy like Anson Williams or Christopher Knight on the show. There was no way any boy would think of me as anything but a little kid in those outfits.

TIME FOR SCHOOL

California State law requires shows to provide teachers on the set for child actors when they're working—somehow four hours of school and a lunch break had to be squeezed into my working day. It didn't have to be four consecutive hours, but no "school session" could be shorter than twenty minutes. Since filming involves a lot of waiting while lights and cameras are repositioned, there were times when I'd just run up and study with the teacher in this teeny little converted dressing room for twenty minutes and then run back when they were ready for the shot. It would get pretty confusing, but the producers of the show tried to arrange my schedule so that I didn't go totally crazy.

Most of the time I was the only student in my set teacher's class. And although there sometimes were other kids on the show, they were usually studying different things, so we all had to have individual instruction. It might sound great to be the only kid in class—you get all the attention and help. On the other hand I could never get away with being unprepared!

Portia, my teacher on the set, was really terrific, and I could always count on her to explain stuff I didn't understand. I guess sometimes I drove her a little crazy. I remember when I was taking a physiology course and I had to dissect a cat. I was carrying it around with me in a plastic bag from home to work to school. Everybody always turned a little green when they saw it. I thought it would be a great joke to put it on the covered serving platter that would be brought to a guest star's dinner table during a scene in one episode. I couldn't wait to see her face when she lifted the cover! Somehow Portia heard about my idea, and I didn't get to do it. But I still think it would have been funny.

There were days when I had very little, or even nothing, to shoot and then I could go to all my classes at my regular school. It's hard to keep up with school life when you're not there very often, so I tried to get there as much as I could. And during the hiatus—most shows shut down production for a month or so each year—I got to go to school every day.

As far as school was concerned, everybody tried to make things work smoothly, but there were times when things got mixed up. One year the teacher at my regular school gave me my assignment for the semester project so I could do it while I was on a cruise. I explained the project to Portia, who was going along—she always had to be there while I was working, whether or not it was in the studio or on a trip. I worked very hard on that project, and Portia read up about it so she could give me classes to cover the right material. And then when I got back, it turned out that the teacher had given me the wrong assignment! I had to make up the whole semester in that class, which meant I never had a break from schoolwork for two whole years!

My workday had to end by four in the afternoon, but that didn't mean that I could just kick back then and relax. I had a tutor in the evenings to help me keep up when I was taking five major courses in school. Besides that, I had to find time for voice and dance classes and, of course, for talking to my friends on thc phone!

PARTIES CAN BE A PART OF WORK, TOO

Lots of people think that movie and TV stars spend all their time going to glamorous parties and having fun. It's true that I go to quite a few parties and I've always thought they were fun. I enjoy getting dressed up and I'm just as star-struck as anyone else. It's great when I find myself seated at the same table as a really famous actor or actress. I was so excited when I got to meet Bob Hope, and in 1984 I went to the White House for the Christmas tree-lighting ceremony. Meeting the President and Mrs. Reagan was just about the most wonderful experience of my life. And since *Eight Is Enough* was one of my favorite shows ever, it was a thrill to meet people like Willie Ames and Grant Goodeve. I felt I was really in the presence of stars, even though I was already on TV myself.

But the events I go to are pretty much divided into "social" parties and "work" parties. Social parties are just what they sound like—a chance to get together with friends either from school or from work.

The ABC Fall Preview party, the Boys' Club Award Dinner, and the Amy Karen Cancer Fund Rainbow Ball are examples of work parties. I know it sounds strange, but I really am working when I attend these. Of course, we're not filming at these events; it's just that I'm there as a representative of the cast of *The Love Boat*. I might have to give out an award or make a little speech—it isn't as if I can just go and hang out with my friends and have a good time doing what I want.

I practically never take a date to these parties because he wouldn't have a very good time sitting alone at our table while I was off being interviewed. I used to go with my mom, but now I usually go with other kids my age who work in television. For instance, I went to a Rainbow Ball with Jimmy Osmond, Kim Fields, Glenn Scarpelli, and Lauri Hendler. Or I go by myself.

Sometimes it's hard to make myself talk to people I've never met before—I'm always afraid I'll say something dumb. But I'm there as part of my job, and once I get started, I end up having a good time. It sure helps when there are a lot of gorgeous guys there like John Travolta to look at!

In addition to work parties, I do a lot of other kinds of appearances. Most of these are for different charities. One project I've been very involved in is Mrs. Reagan's Action program, which is designed to steer kids away from drugs, and I've also done a lot of work for the Girl Scouts, the Boys' Clubs of America, and the Amy Karen Cancer Fund. I also appear on telethons to raise money for research on diseases like cerebral palsy and multiple sclerosis and for organizations like the March of Dimes, Easter Seals, and Variety Clubs.

Variety Club work has taken me all over the country. Once I was in Kansas City with Glenn Scarpelli for a Variety Club telethon, and we got snowed in. There was no way to get back to Los Angeles, and I was supposed to be at the studio at seven-thirty the next morning! I was frantic, but Mom called the studio and explained what had happened. They weren't too pleased, but luckily they were able to change the schedule and shoot my scenes later in the day. I flew out of Kansas City in the morning, and there was a limousine waiting for me at the airport in Los Angeles, so I managed to get to the studio just in time—but it was a close call!

IS IT ALL WORTH IT? YOU BET!

There are so many wonderful things about being in show business, but like any other kind of work, it has its drawbacks too. One thing that we all find a little difficult is that we never know until late in the year whether *The Love Boat* is going to be picked up for the next season. Of course, we're lucky to be on a show that's been successful for so long, but still, it's hard to have that uncertainty hanging over our heads.

Sometimes it's not so great to be recognized everywhere as "that girl on *The Love Boat*," and there are people who get some weird ideas about someone like me. My trailer at the studio, which is my dressing room and my home away from home, has been broken into a few times, and it really upset me. Not very much was stolen, because usually there's nothing much there except a bunch of magazines and books, but it made me feel that my privacy had been invaded, and I have little enough privacy as it is!

And although I love my work, sometimes it's hard to keep on smiling. When we were in Copenhagen, we were shooting a scene at the Tivoli Gardens, a famous amusement park. It's a fabulous place, and I'd have loved to explore all of it, but unfortunately it was raining really hard, and the scene took the entire day to get done. I looked like a drowned cat, and my shoes were soaked completely through so my socks and feet were wet and cold after the first hour. What I wanted to do was go inside somewhere and curl up in front of a nice warm fire. Instead, all of us had to keep going and pretend we were having the best time of our lives!

For the last few years I've had a pretty hectic schedule, and sometimes I felt as if I never had even a minute to call my own. There were times when I wanted to just daydream or stare into space or not talk to anyone if I was feeling a little down. Probably every busy teenager feels this way, whether it's from being on a television show or from juggling school, extracurricular activities, and an afterschool job.

The thing that helped me most when I felt like this was realizing that I had chosen to be on the show—it was something I really wanted. I mean, if it had really been too much for me, I could always have quit. We all make choices about how we spend our time, and frequently those choices mean giving up other things. I decided that the things I'd chosen to do meant more to me than the free time I had to do without. I like my life real well—at least most of the time.

Dear Jill,

I started high school this year, and I've already been asked to be the lead in the school play. Ever since I can remember, I have wanted to be an actress and anytime there was a chance to play a part, even if it was one of the shepherds in the church Christmas pageant, I did it because I just love being on stage! My mom and dad think I'm pretty good (not that I mean to brag) and they say that they'll be happy for me if I get to be a real actress, because that's what I want to do. But I'm not lucky like you. I live in a small town in the Midwest nowhere near a big city. And there's no way I can go and live in Hollywood or New York or anyplace like that. How can I get work in the movies or television from way out here?

Sandy S.

Dear Sandy,

First of all, don't feel desperate—it sounds like you already have a lot of things going for you. You're lucky to have a family that's supportive of your dreams, and you're also lucky to have gotten some acting experience already. I think experience is the most important thing for any aspiring actress, so keep on doing as many shows as you can. I'll bet there's a college near where you live. Try getting in touch with whatever theater department they have and see if you can work on their productions, even if you can't be on stage. Or see if you can find a community theater group. And be creative—maybe there's a fund-raising group that's putting on a show of some kind, or maybe you can talk them into doing one!

It's not too early to talk to your guidance counselor at school and start finding out about the colleges and universities that have strong theater programs. If possible, you should apply to these schools. You'll get good training and experience, and you'll also be in an atmosphere where you'll find out about how things are done—how to get an agent and so on.

The only other thing I can suggest is to try and get an agent now. But don't be disappointed, though, if this doesn't get results. You have to understand that there are an awful lot of kids who want to be in show business, and there really aren't that many parts available for young people.

From your letter you sound like a girl with good sense and determination, so I know that if you don't find an agent right away, you'll go on acting in high school and college. I think that's the best way to help make your dream come true. And since theater people think it's bad luck to say "Good luck," I'll say "Break a leg!"

Chapter 3

All in the Family

I GUESS MOST kids really love their families, but I think mine is extraspecial. There are five in my family—my mom and dad; my older brother, Chuck; and my older sister, Nancy. And of course, me—I'm the baby. My brother is five years older than I am, and my sister is four years older, so as we were growing up they were always way ahead of me in school. That's why we didn't have the kinds of fights I hear about from my friends who have brothers and sisters closer to their age. After all, I was still in grade school when they were in high school. Whatever the reason, we've always gotten along together well.

As I said before, we used to live in Livermore, in northern California, and I liked living there when I was a kid. When I first started working in Los Angeles, we commuted back and forth, but eventually my mom and I had to move down here. By that time Chuck and Nancy had graduated from high school.

Dad still lives in our old house in Livermore because his business is up there, and he doesn't want to give that up. I love going back there, and when I was younger, we used to fly up for weekends a lot. That's harder now because of my busy schedule, so Dad comes to Los Angeles for holidays and as many weekends as he can.

BEING A WORKING KID

My whole family has always been really supportive and understanding about my career. When I read books about other families in show business, I feel really fortunate that we've never had the kinds of family disputes and unhappiness that sometimes seem to happen. Neither Chuck nor Nancy ever wanted to be in the performing side of show business, so I don't think they felt jealous when I started working on television. Still, I'm sure they must have been a little resentful because I got a lot of attention. But they never acted as if they were feeling overshadowed or anything. In fact, they both still treat me like any older brother and sister treat their baby sister!

I'm so grateful to my parents for everything they've done to help me. I know they gave up a lot to let me have my career. They don't get to see each other as much as they used to since my mom had to move with me to Los Angeles. And my mom eventually had to give up most of her social life in our old town and make a whole new batch of friends here.

In addition, my mom has had to be with me on the set most of the time when I was working, and she used to accompany me to all the work functions I had to go to. It can't have been a whole lot of fun for her to work her life around my schedule.

On the other hand being with me at work made it easy for her to see how to keep me in line. Whenever I gave her a bad time, all she had to say was, "If you don't shape up, we'll just forget this television business and go home to Livermore." That was all I needed!

Don't get me wrong—it wasn't all bad for my mom. She made lots of friends at the studio, and she got to go with us on all our cruises. I think she's enjoyed the traveling as much as I have, and some of the things that have happened have been pretty funny—at least she thought so!

She always likes to tell the story of what happened once when we were in Australia. Mom was going out to a movie with some other people, and I was spending the evening at the hotel with my set teacher, Portia. Before she left, Mom said, "Be sure not to double-lock the door of our room when you go to bed—I'll never be able to wake you up."

I said okay, but after Portia went to her room about ten o'clock, I felt nervous. I was planning to stay awake and watch TV in bed anyway, so I went ahead and put the chain on the door. The next thing I knew, I was sitting up in bed and there was this whole crowd of people staring at me.

Of course, what had happened was that I fell asleep, and Mom was right—she wasn't able to wake me up. I found out later that she'd been banging on the door and yelling to me for quite a while. She woke up some other people, and they came out into the hall and tried to help her wake me up, but nothing worked. Then she got really nervous, and she thought I must be sick or kidnapped or dead. So she got the hotel security man and the manager and who knows who else, and they came and cut the chain off the door with a saw. Meanwhile she was calling to me the whole time, and I didn't hear a thing! I guess I'm a pretty sound sleeper.

When the door was finally open, Mom ran in and there I was, curled up on the bed with all the pillows around me. But she didn't wake me up right away. Instead, she went out and got all the people who'd been helping her and brought them in to see me—and *then* she woke me up!

HAVING A REGULAR CHILDHOOD

I've wanted to be an actress practically since I could understand what an actress was. But my parents really wanted me to have a normal childhood, so they didn't encourage me a lot when I was little. I did all the kinds of things most little girls do, like being in Brownies and Girl Scouts and taking all kinds of lessons. I was pretty good at gymnastics, and I was on a swim team, which I really enjoyed. Besides that I played soccer and took ballet lessons.

But all along I was determined to be an actress, so when I was eight, I sent a letter and my pictures to an agent all on my own. I guess that made my parents realize that I wanted this more than anything in the world and was willing to work hard for it. After that they felt they just couldn't stand in the way if I was offered acting jobs. They thought I should have the opportunity to try to make my dream become reality, and it would be unfair not to give me that chance. I'm sure glad they did!

But even after I started acting, my parents tried to keep my life as normal as possible. My mom spent a lot of extra time with me, because she had to come with me to Los Angeles whenever I was working. But my mom and dad are real big on treating all us kids the same. For instance, my birthday and my sister's birthday are only three days apart, but our parents never made us celebrate them together. And we took turns every year to have a really big party with some kind of a theme, like a pirate party.

Here's another example of how we kids were all treated the same. When I was twelve, I really wanted to have my ears pierced. But Nancy hadn't been allowed to have her ears pierced until she was fourteen. I was working in Los Angeles, and Mom made me call up Nancy to ask her whether she minded if I had mine done two years earlier than she had! Of course, Nancy didn't care, but it let me know that I wasn't going to get away with anything.

EVERYONE HAS RULES AND REGULATIONS

Like every other teenager in the world, I've had to follow lots of rules that my parents felt were important. I guess most of them make sense when I think about them, but sometimes I find them pretty annoying. For instance, it seems as if every time I sit down to watch something on TV, my mom says, "Isn't there something you ought to be doing?" or "Don't you have something to do?" Sometimes she's right—I should be studying or getting dressed because I'm supposed to be going out soon. But other times it makes me wonder if she thinks watching TV doesn't count as "doing something."

Up until fairly recently I've had curfew hours, and I had to be in earlier than a lot of my friends did. For me it wasn't much of a problem because I'm usually ready to fall in bed by eleven o'clock or so anyway. I'm so used to getting up early and cramming every waking minute full that I'm exhausted long before midnight. When I was in junior high and early high school, I had to be in by a certain time; then I got to be a junior, and my parents were a little more lenient.

I know a lot of my friends didn't like their parents' telling them when they had to be home. I didn't mind all that much. Maybe that's because I would have probably been home by then anyway. And partly I'm sure it was because my mom was pretty good about not making an issue out of it. A lot of what I do at night is work-related, and if a business party ran a little late, I could just call my mom and tell her when I'd be home.

Of course, she would wait up for me. She still does! But now she tries to make it look casual. She sits on the couch in the living room with her feet up watching television. From where she is she can see the front door just by turning her head. So when I come in, she just glances over and says, "Oh, hi, honey!" in this surprised voice, like she wasn't even expecting me. But I'm not fooled. Actually, though, it makes me feel good that she still worries about me.

THE MOTHER-DAUGHTER CONFLICT

I don't want to make it sound as though Mom and I have an absolutely perfect relationship or that we never disagree about anything. Naturally that's not true. Sometimes I think she's going to nag me to death! Like when I'm rushing out of the house and she says, "Wait a minute! Fix your face, comb your hair, and put on a bra!" I mean, I'm usually only going down to the market to pick up some milk or something, and it wouldn't matter if I had a bra on or not!

But most of the time it's easier to do it her way than to have a big discussion about it.

Mom and I are both strong people—you might even say stubborn—and we don't see everything the same way all the time. One thing we don't always agree about is my clothes. I love clothes and I especially love shopping for them. And when I had to wear things that were much too young for me on the show, I really enjoyed getting outfits for myself that were more sophisticated. But sometimes what I thought was sophisticated my mom thought was just plain too old for me. She might say, "Well, I think that doesn't really suit you," or something gentle like that. But other times she was much more blunt. She'd say, "That makes you look about twenty, and you're only sixteen. I suppose when you're twenty you'll be dressing like you're thirty." I never did come up with a good answer to that one!

Once when I was looking for something to wear to an awards dinner, I found this fabulous dress. It was blue and kind of tight-fitting, except that it flared out at the bottom. What I really loved about it was that the whole top was covered with sequins. I knew I just had to have it! So I dragged Mom down to the store and tried it on. It looked great on me, but I knew I was in trouble when she got this pained look on her face and covered her eyes with her hand. Before she even opened her mouth, I knew the answer was no. And discussing it wasn't going to help!

Often, though, Mom and I do talk things over after we've both had time to cool off. And many times we can reach a compromise if we're both willing to give in a little.

I bet there isn't a teenager in the world who hasn't had arguments with her parents. And sometimes you get so frustrated that you just want to scream. If you can make yourself calm down, though, you can sit down with your mom or dad and try to discuss the problem in a rational way. Even if you don't convince them you're right, they're likely to think you're handling it in a mature way and that might make them more willing to listen to your point of view the next time.

That sounds like a terrific way to do things, doesn't it? But I have to tell you that I don't always succeed in following my own advice, even when I've got it all worked out in my mind.

For example, take my diet. I'm very serious about it, and when I'm dieting, I really stick to it. So how do you think I feel when I'm in the kitchen and my mom calls to me, "What are you doing in there, Jill?"

I say in this really cold voice, "I'm *just* getting a glass of water, if that's okay." I know that sounds a little snippy, but her question really makes me annoyed. I feel that my mom should trust me not to eat when I'm not supposed to, and I think she should understand that I have to do it on my own.

I know she's only saying these things because she truly cares about me and she wants the best for me in every way. All mothers feel that way. But I'm not a child anymore, and I have to prove to myself and to her that I can do things on my own. She knows this too, but it's hard for her to stop watching over me.

TAKING CHARGE OF YOUR OWN LIFE

As teenagers, one of the things we're working toward is being responsible for ourselves. This was so important to me that when I made up my mind to lose weight, I was lucky to be able to go away for two weeks. I wasn't sure I could do it on my own, but I thought if I didn't try, I never *would* know.

Surely you don't have to do anything as drastic as getting out of your house in order to create your own space. Every teenager can find an opportunity to make a decision about some aspect of her life and then carry it through. It's awfully easy to let other people keep taking responsibility for you. But if you don't do anything until you've been nagged to death about it, you won't ever know how much you could have accomplished on your own.

I'M TRYING TO BE PERFECT—GIVE ME A BREAK!

It seems that we're all trying to live up to someone's expectations of us—parents', friends', teachers', and our own. And there's nothing wrong with that as long as what's expected of us is somewhere in the realm of possibility. But sometimes it seems that no matter how hard we try, we can't measure up.

Has this ever happened to you? Your teacher calls you in after school and says, "You only got a B on your math test, and I know you're an A student. I know you can do better." But what's going on in your mind is this: *I studied my brains out for this test and I think I did pretty well to get a B. I'm trying as hard as I can. How can I do more?*

Or your best friend says, "I'm so upset about breaking up with my boyfriend, and you don't even have time to listen. A real friend would care more." And you're thinking: *Gosh, I've already talked to you for three nights in a row for three hours on the phone, my parents have cut me down to five minutes per phone call, and I haven't started writing my term paper that's due the day after tomorrow. How much more can I give you right now?*

And as for your parents—they often seem to expect you to be perfect in every way. Sometimes my mom drives me wild. I'm trying to be perfect and she says I'm not, and I get so offended. I'm trying to do it right, and then when she sighs and makes a weird comment, it just makes me want to cry.

What to do about this? Well, I shut my eyes and say, "Leave me alone. I don't want to talk about it." But I'm not sure that's such a good solution. My friend Nicky goes into her Camille act—she puts her hand to her forehead and sighs while big tears drip down her cheeks. I don't think that works much better than my method!

Actually it does help to say straight out "Hey, come on, I'm really *not* perfect, I'm a regular person like anyone else." Sometimes this makes your parents see that you can't be everything they want you to be. But it probably won't last. By the next week they'll be back to asking why you can't get straight A's, have a whole crowd of wonderful friends, play the violin solo in the school concert, keep your room neat, and get all your other chores done at the same time.

At those times maybe the only thing to do is remember

that you're their kid, and of course, they think there's no other kid in the world as wonderful as you.

KEEPING AN OPEN MIND

Is your mother Dear Abby, Ann Landers, and Miss Manners all rolled into one? Does she have advice for every possible situation, even ones that have never come up and never will? Welcome to the club!

Most mothers have a lot more advice to offer than anyone can use. I've often felt that Mom gave me many more words of wisdom than I ever wanted to hear. I went through a phase of just shutting my ears. If it was her idea, I didn't even want to try it.

But not too long ago my sister, Nancy, said to me, "You know, I did something really stupid and if I'd listened to Mom, it wouldn't have happened. I wish I'd paid attention to what she said." That really made me stop and think!

After all, your own mom is certainly going to give you the best advice she can. She cares about you, and she wants your life to be terrific. And besides, she was a teenager herself. Maybe her own life experiences have taught her a lot of things that can be really helpful to you. At least you could give it a listen without getting bent out of shape the minute she starts talking. After my chat with my sister, I decided I was going to try to listen more to what my mom had to say—maybe I'd learn something!

GROWING INTO A NEW ROLE

As I look back over my early teen years I can see that many of the decisions I made and battles I fought were my way of reaching toward my own independence as a person. I never had this as a planned-out goal in my mind—I always just figured that growing up was what happened to you as you got older. Only recently has it occurred to me that moving toward adulthood is a process in which I am an active participant—in fact, the star performer!

Each step in this process brings its own changes. I'm

sure every teenager goes through these same steps at her own pace and in her own way. Finally, after several years of learning about ourselves and finding out how to handle responsibility for our own lives, we'll be ready to leave our parents and go out on our own.

Moving out of the family orbit is scary for me, and now as I begin to think about finding a place of my own, sometimes I panic a little. My mom and I are so close, and we're such good friends. She still comes with me to parties that friends in the *Love Boat* cast and crew give, and we have a great time. She's a fun date! We can sit around and dish and talk about people.

It's hard for her and it's hard for me to think about moving away from home. We've been together so much, and if she's not with me, sometimes I'm afraid I'll fail. One week I feel like a little kid still clinging to her; the next week I can't wait to be on my own.

Do all teenagers feel like this when they're through with high school and preparing themselves for the next stage of their lives? Maybe I won't be ready to move out, but the only way I'll find out is if I try it. And sometimes there needs to be a break between parents and kids.

What I look forward to when I live by myself is just being alone. I'd like to come home and relax and not have to talk about what went on all day. I'm getting to the point where I need my space, and my parents probably need their space too.

When you have a wonderful family like mine, it's sad to think about leaving them. But that's part of growing up, and it's exciting to look forward to being independent. And I know that my family will always be there for me when I need them, just as they always have been.

Dear Jill,

I'm really upset and I don't know what to do. For the past few months my parents have been fighting all the time, and I'm scared that they might be getting a divorce. I feel as if it's all my fault, and I need to know what to do about it. Please help me!

Nicole T.

Dear Nicole,

The main thing you have to know right away is that if your parents are thinking about a divorce, it's *not* your fault. Your parents are grown-up people, and whatever problems they have are between them. No matter how good or how bad you are, it won't change their decision. You don't have the power either to make them get a divorce or to make them stay together.

People can change, and their feelings for each other can change too. Put yourself in their place—would you want to live with someone you were unhappy with? I think you should understand that they have to live their own lives.

Of course, you'd like them to stay together, and maybe they will be able to work out their problems. You'll just have to wait and see. But in the meantime, if you're feeling upset and scared, you should talk to them. I think a good thing to say is something like, "Mom (or Dad), I know you're having problems, but I want you to know that I love you both." This can let them know that you're concerned and open the door for communication between you.

Dear Jill,

My parents are so strict, you wouldn't believe it! It seems as if I can't do anything my friends are allowed to do. It's not fair, but I can't seem to talk them into changing their minds. Why can't they see that I'm old enough to have more freedom?

Kathy L.

Dear Kathy,

I think this must be a common problem because I've heard a lot of girls complain about the very same thing. Maybe you're overreacting a little. Are you sure that *all* your friends' parents are so much more lenient than yours? Check it out—you may be surprised at what you find out.

But if your parents really are stricter than others, I think you might try to introduce them to your friends. When you have the gang over to your house for an afternoon or evening, it gives your mom and dad a chance to see that they're nice kids, not a bunch of wild hoodlums! At least this will reassure them about your safety.

Another thing that helps is to introduce your parents to your friends' parents, if they don't already know them. That way they'll be able to talk things over with adults who might convince them they're worrying more than they need to.

Maybe the problem is that when you discuss your friends' parents' rules with your own parents, you get upset or hysterical, and then they think you're still too young for more freedom. Try saying something like this: "I know you worry about me, but I'm a pretty good kid—I don't take drugs or get into trouble. The restrictions you impose on me make me feel like an outsider with my friends. It seems as if you're not giving me the right to grow up in a normal way in our community. I wish you'd try giving me a little more leeway so I can have a chance to show you I can handle the responsibility and I can be trusted."

Remember, when you talk it over with your parents, don't act smart about it. That never works, and it leads to the wrong reaction every time! Try to be as calm as you can, and if it works and they relax the rules a little bit, don't take advantage, or you'll be right back where you started!

Dear Jill,

This might sound a little weird, but I know my mom likes my sister much better than me. She always has time to do stuff for my sister, but when I ask her for anything, she's always too busy. It makes me feel terrible. Aren't parents supposed to love all their kids the same?

Ellen M.

Dear Ellen,

It might help if you can admit to yourself that you feel jealous of your sister and her relationship with your mom. Then you can talk to your mother without sounding as if you're blaming her for the whole situation. You might say something like, "I don't know whether it's me or what, but I feel I'm being neglected. If it's me, I wish you'd help me find out why I feel this way. If not, I wish you'd show me more attention, because I think right now I need it." This will let her know how you feel without making her feel guilty about it, and it should lead to a discussion that will make you feel better.

However, I think that sometimes, even though a parent truly loves her child, their personalities don't quite mesh. It's probably just a phase, and after a while you'll be best friends again. But if this is what's going on between you and your mother, you might try to find another adult you can talk to in the meantime. Maybe a friend's mother or a counselor at school can be helpful. Tell this person your problem—then ask if it's okay for you to talk to her. But don't overdo it or pester the person too much, because it can put her in a difficult position.

Chapter 4

Friendship Makes the World Go Round

FRIENDS ARE IMPORTANT to everyone, but somehow, when you're a teenager, it seems as if you can't live without them. Who else will understand your jokes and giggle with you over your most embarrassing moments? And who else will sympathize when you don't have a date for the Valentine Dance or you can't be in the class play because you got the flu?

Friends occupy a special place in your life. They're not members of your family—you get to choose them for yourself. And you don't have to like them all the same amount or exactly the same way. I have some friends who I wouldn't really trust with everything. But they're fun to go out and do stuff with, and I don't mind that I can't always say how I really feel about things when I'm with them.

Then I have other friends I can share just about anything with. These are my best friends. I know they like me just the way I am. I don't have to try to impress them or be on my best behavior with them. My being on television doesn't have anything to do with our friendship—they're friends with me, Jill Whelan, not with Vicky Stubing from *The Love Boat*.

I think everybody needs at least one best friend! The person I think of as my best friend is Nicky, and I don't know what I'd do if I didn't have a friend like her. We call each other on the phone a lot, even if we don't have anything very important to say. We call each other "baby." I'm sure our phone conversations sound really weird to other people, with these two teenage girls saying *baby* all the time, but we know what we mean! That's one of the great things about a really close friend—after a while you know each other so well that you don't have to explain what you mean all the time. It's as if you have your own private code for communicating with each other. And that can make you feel that even when everything else is going wrong in your life, there's one person out there who really understands you.

WHEN FRIENDS DISAPPOINT YOU, IT HURTS

Sometimes a friend can turn out to be different from what you thought she was. And that can be very upsetting, especially if you were very close. It's hard to deal with the fact that someone you thought liked you a whole lot doesn't seem to like you so much anymore.

I used to have a friend—I'll call her Kay—when I still lived in Livermore. But after I started working in television, she didn't seem so friendly anymore. It's true that at that time of my life I was in Los Angeles a lot, but I was still registered in school in Livermore. I went to class there whenever I was home and besides, I was always home on weekends. So I didn't see why we couldn't still be friends.

Kay was acting pretty cool toward me, and finally I asked her what was the matter. And she said she thought I had changed. I was really upset. We'd been best friends since second grade, and I didn't feel I had changed toward her at all.

I tried to keep on being friendly, hoping she'd see that I was still the same as I'd always been. But it didn't seem to help. She acted more and more distant and made a point of shutting me out of her life. At one point Kay and another friend of hers told me that they'd made up a secret code word, and I couldn't be their friend until I guessed it. I stayed up all night trying to figure out what it was, but I never did. (Later on I realized that they probably never really had a code word at all. Or if they did, they probably would have kept changing it if I'd guessed it right. The whole thing was just a way of letting me know they didn't want to be friends with me.)

But when this was going on, I didn't know what to do, and finally I got so unhappy about it that I talked to my mom. After I told her what had been happening, she said, "You haven't changed, but Kay has."

When I heard her say that, all of a sudden I knew she was right. I don't know why I couldn't come up with that answer myself, but looking at it in that light, I felt so relieved. Of course, I felt sad, too, because I was losing a friend who had been so close to me for so long.

I spent the next few days thinking about it, and I never did know exactly what had gone wrong between Kay and me. I don't know if she was jealous of my being an actress or if she just assumed that because I was working on a TV show, I'd be real full of myself and wouldn't have time for my old friends anymore. I guess sometimes people are so afraid of getting hurt themselves that they pull away before it has a chance to happen. And it's always easier to blame dissolving friendships on the other person.

People do change over time, and you can't always stay friends with someone forever. Maybe Kay and I would have grown apart as we got older and found out that we had different interests. But at the time I felt very hurt. I wish she'd given me a chance to show her that I was still the same person I'd always been.

I realize now, though, that Mom was right. Kay had changed and there was nothing I could do about that. There are times in everyone's life when a friend disappoints you or makes it clear that she's not your friend anymore. There's no use blaming yourself when that happens, or making yourself unhappy about it. Just remember that there will be other people who will appreciate you and value you as a friend.

TRYING TOO HARD

Sometimes you get really worried that people won't like you or want to be friends with you. Feeling that way is terrible, and it can make you try to act different from your normal self. You may be thinking that people will like you better if you pretend to be another kind of person.

I guess I fell into that trap myself. After what happened with Kay, I got very worried that other kids in my old school would stop being friends with me too. So I became the class clown—always joking around, always cheerful, always being a good sport and everybody's buddy. I tried to be friends with everyone in the whole class, even if I had nothing much in common with the person and we'd never been friends before.

In a way this worked fine. Most of the kids seemed to like me and think that I was fun to have around. But after a while I felt as if I were playing a role all the time. And I didn't know if anyone would like me if I stopped acting the clown and started being myself again.

I think the worst thing you can do is to try to change yourself to please your friends or to hang on to a friendship. It makes you feel bad about yourself, because what you're really saying is that you're not a likable person and to make people like you you have to become a different person. That's a pretty terrible thing to feel about yourself.

And in the long run I think trying to change yourself into someone different doesn't actually help. You just end up feeling that you're trapped in the part you're playing, and you're afraid to stop playing it. That kind of thing makes you tense and nervous and basically pretty unhappy. It's all part of the same thing—when you feel good about yourself and when you understand that you have good things to offer other people, even if they're not the same good things as someone else has, other people are likely to feel good about you too. There's a book called *How to Be Your Own Best Friend*, and I always thought that was such a neat concept.

After all, if a person doesn't think much of herself, she's likely to be worrying all the time about what other people think of her and trying to cover up her own feelings—she won't have very much energy to spare for being a good friend to you or anyone else.

FRIENDS CAN TAKE ADVANTAGE OF YOU

Sometimes all of us wonder if some of the people we think of as our friends really care about us. I bet everyone has had the experience of feeling that a pal is only interested in what you can do for her. For instance, you might have a friend who calls you every night to ask about the homework assignment in your English class. After a while you realize that she's not just asking you what the assignment is—she's asking you how to do it, and you're spending two hours on the phone doing her work for her.

You think, Well, of course I'll help her—what are friends for? But then you might start to notice that she never calls you about anything else and somehow she forgets to invite you to her parties. This can make you feel that you're being used—and you're right.

Maybe there are people who use you for other reasons. If you have more spending money than the other kids you know, you may find that you're always invited along to the local hamburger hangout, but when there's a get-together at someone's house, you're not included. Of course, it's not nice for people to do that to you. But stop and be honest with yourself. Have you been trying to buy the friendship of a particular group by always offering to pay for their snacks? When you think it over, you may decide that these people aren't the ones you want to be friends with anyway.

Or how about this one? Your older brother is captain of the football team, and suddenly you've got a lot of new girlfriends who stop by your house to see you—but only when your brother is home! You can't blame them for trying. And it may turn out that some of them become good friends with you. But don't be too disappointed if others drop you as soon as your brother goes off to college.

There are times when friends take advantage of you

without really meaning to. My brother, Chuck, knew a guy in high school who called him all the time on the phone. This guy—I'll call him Dan—felt that Chuck was the only person he could talk to. It was kind of funny. Chuck would put down the phone and go downstairs to watch TV, and my mom would pick it up and hear Dan talking away. She'd say, "Chuck, Dan is on the phone!" And Chuck always said, "Yeah, I know, I'll be there in a minute." Then he'd come up and pick up the phone and say "Uh-huh," and then put it down on the counter again and go make himself a sandwich. He might pick it up in a few minutes and say, "Yeah, right," and then go do something else.

But it was kind of pathetic at the same time. Dan was so wrapped up in himself and his problems that he never even noticed that all Chuck did was say "Uh-huh" into the phone. He certainly never wanted to hear about Chuck's problems!

If you're a good listener, it's easy to get trapped in this situation. And if you're a kind-hearted type, you feel bad if you don't keep on listening to all their troubles. But a person like this is taking advantage of you. You're spending all your time listening to their stories, and they never have time to listen to yours. Not only that—your listening isn't doing any good. A person like this never keeps quiet long enough to hear what you have to say, so you might as well be a tape recorder for all the good you're doing. You may start to feel that your time is more valuable than that. But still, this person probably says something like "You're the only friend I have," so you can't just tell her to shut up.

I think the only thing you can do is try to set some limits. You could say, "Gosh, my mom won't let me talk longer than five minutes on the phone" or "I'm just getting ready to jump into the shower and I can't talk." There isn't any need to be rude or to cut this person off completely. And after all, she may just be going through a bad time, and in a month or so she'll calm down and listen to you now and then. Friendship is a two-way street; don't put yourself in the position of either giving or taking all the time.

NEW FACES, NEW POSSIBILITIES

Starting at a new school is exciting, but it's also really scary. Will anyone talk to you and help you find your way around? Will you make a fool of yourself by wearing the wrong kind of clothes? Or will you sound really out of it, as though you don't know what's going on with the social scene?

You can't help worrying about stuff like this, and I guess everybody does it. I know that when I started going to school in Los Angeles, I just wanted to blend in with the other kids. I tried to act like everyone else and I made an effort not to be the center of attention, because I didn't want them to think I was showing off.

It was easier for me in some ways than it had been at my old school in Livermore. Although none of the other kids in my new class were working like I was, some of their parents were in the television or movie business. In fact, a few of the parents were famous names in show business, so nobody was overwhelmed by what I was doing or thought it was a big deal. They all understood that I came to school whenever I could—that is, whenever I had a block of time that I wasn't needed on the set. I really preferred going to school when it was possible, rather than always having classes with my set teacher in that little converted dressing room. And I think my friends at school understood that and they didn't think I was getting away with anything, although sometimes they would tease me and say things like, "I didn't know you were still going to this school—you're never here!"

Another thing that made it easier when I started at my new school was that I'd met a girl who lived down the street from the friend Mom and I were staying with in Los Angeles, and she went to that school. As a matter of fact, she was one of the reasons I decided to go there—she'd told me a lot about it, and she made it sound pretty good. We got to be very good friends. In fact, it was Nicky and she's still my best friend!

Even though getting to know a whole new group of kids was kind of hard, I knew it was up to me to make the most of the situation. How I approached it would have a lot to do with whether it was a good or a not-so-good experience. But I was nervous about it, and I tried to think of some way to make it easier and less scary.

Finally I decided to ask if I could work on the theater production at the school during the summer before I started my first year there. I knew I would feel comfortable working on a show because I had done it so many times before at community theaters in northern California. And I thought it would be a good way to meet some of the kids from the school who, like me, were also in love with acting and the theater. I'm really glad I did it, because it worked out very well. I ended up performing in one show—I was one of Annie's younger sisters in *Annie Get Your Gun*—and doing the lights for *The Jungle Book*. And the best part of it was that I met a whole bunch of kids, so I didn't feel like a total stranger when I started classes in the fall.

If I were giving someone advice about starting out at a new school, I'd tell her to get involved right away in some kind of extracurricular activity. It doesn't have to be theater—it might be a particular sport or a tutoring program for younger or disabled kids, or a hiking club, or just about anything. The point is that it's a great way to meet people who are interested in the same things you are, and somehow it's not nearly so scary when you only have a small group to deal with at first. Then when you actually start school, you'll know a little bit about what you're doing, and there will be a few familiar, friendly faces in the halls as you try to find your way around a new building!

ALL KINDS OF FRIENDS

One of the nice things about working on *The Love Boat* is that I've made so many wonderful friends over the years. I'm the only teenager who works regularly on the show, so none of my friends there are my age. I think that's kind of neat. Having friends of all different ages has taught me a lot about life—and it's a lot of fun too!

As I mentioned before, one of my best friends on the show is Margie. She does the body makeup, and she's been in the film business longer than I have. I won't tell you how old she is because she'd be mad at me! But when I tell you that her husband, who's a wonderful guy, is Santa Claus in the Los Angeles Christmas Parade every year, you'll know that Margie is just a *teeny* bit older than I am! But it's funny. When we're fooling around at work and giggling at some dumb joke, I feel like she's about the same age as me. I can talk to her about anything at all.

I've learned, too, that guys can be good friends. A lot of the cast and crew of the show are men, and I feel really close to some of them. This is important to me because we work together almost every day, and of course, when we go on cruises we're all traveling together for six weeks.

It feels great to walk onto the set and know that my buddies are there, ready to give me a smile and a hug or a sympathetic ear. I've heard that some shows don't have this kind of friendly working atmosphere. On some of the sets it seems there's a lot of competition for the limelight, and a lot of showing off and backbiting and undercutting the other actors. I'd really hate that. It seems kind of stupid, too, because if you work with the same people all the time, it's so much nicer if you're all friends and get along well with each other. I'm sure it's not much fun to work on the shows where people don't feel that way. A couple of times people who've done guest spots on *The Love Boat* have commented on how warm and friendly our show seems. They've told me, "You don't know how lucky you are!" But I think I do know, and I really appreciate all the wonderful friends I've made.

HOW DO YOU MEET NEW FRIENDS?

There were only forty kids in my high school class. In some ways that was nice because we all felt relaxed with one another, and everybody knew everybody else. But in some ways it wasn't so great, because there's never anyone new to get to know. And once you know those forty kids, there are bound to be some you really like and some you just don't have much to say to. So you're narrowed down to not very many kids to do things with.

Because of my work schedule, I didn't have much extra

time, and I rarely got a chance to meet other kids my own age outside my school. So when I was offered the opportunity to take part in the debutante season in Los Angeles, I was really happy. (I was a little nervous too!)

The way it worked was that the first time we all got together was at one lady's house. We were supposed to gather there to get packed into cars to go to Lake Arrowhead for a get-acquainted weekend. I looked around at the group, and I didn't know anybody!

At first I just sort of stood around not saying anything and kind of hoping no one would notice me. Then I said to myself, "This is silly." I knew if I kept on that way, I'd have a horrible weekend. So I started introducing myself to some of the other girls. Lots of them seemed to know each other already, but some were like me and didn't know anyone at all. I picked out those people first to do my get-acquainted stuff—I figured they probably felt as uncomfortable as I did and they'd be likely to act friendly to me if I made the first move.

Basically I'm a shy person, so it was difficult for me to make myself get started in that situation. The only thing I could think of was What if they didn't like me? What if I tried to be friendly, and they ignored me? It was pretty scary. But one thing my job on TV has taught me is that people are basically nice. If you act friendly toward them, they're usually going to be friendly back. On the other hand if you let your shyness get the best of you and you sit in a corner not saying anything, they're likely to think that you aren't interested in making friends, and they'll stay away from you too. It turns into a vicious circle.

When I'm in a group of people I don't know, I'm always a little scared. But what I do is pick out someone who looks interesting, take a deep breath, and go over and say, "Hi, I'm Jill." If you smile when you say it, just about anybody will smile back and tell you her name.

If you're really nervous, sometimes it's a good idea to have something to say to this person like "I love your dress—where did you get it?" I did this once when I was on a telethon, and I didn't really know any of the other people. But there was one girl there who was wearing the exact same shoes I was! So I went up to her and said, "You're wearing my shoes!" And we started talking about where we'd bought them and it turned out that she loved shoes almost as much as I do and we had a great time telling each other new places to shop for them. In fact, we got to be pretty good friends after that, and all because we have the same taste in shoes!

Most of the time I find that once I'm over the hurdle of the first hello, it's pretty easy to start up a conversation. I'm always surprised to find out that people who look totally together can have the same problem I do. Maybe everybody feels this way, and some have just learned to hide it better. I always have to remind myself that I've been in these situations before, and things have always worked out fine. I know this in my head, but it doesn't stop me from being nervous all over again every time. I try to remember what I did the last time, and if it worked, I do the same thing again.

You have to figure out what approach works best for you. Obviously if you don't care much about clothes or shoes, you wouldn't feel comfortable asking a stranger about stuff like that. But there's usually *something* you can ask, and most people are flattered when you ask about something they're involved in. Usually they're happy to talk about it. The thing to remember is, if you don't take the risk of making the first move with a new person, you might lose out on meeting a terrific new friend. And if the worst happens and the person you reach out to isn't very friendly, you'll feel embarrassed—but what do you care what a person like that thinks of you?

Just so you know how it turned out, I had a great weekend at Lake Arrowhead, and I got to know the rest of the girls. They were a terrific group, and some of us have become really good friends since then. I was happy that I'd taken the step of doing it in spite of feeling nervous at the beginning.

CLIQUES ARE NO FUN!

When I was younger, I didn't know what the word *clique* meant. But when someone explained the term to me, I knew exactly what they were talking about—I just hadn't known that's what it was called. I guess there are cliques in every school. They have certainly existed in every school I've ever gone to, and they've always been a source of unhappiness and even heartbreak for some people.

I've never been part of a clique, probably because I've always enjoyed having all different kinds of friends. And that's exactly what you can't do if you're in a clique. Of course, everyone is likely to have a special group of friends—I have a bunch of girlfriends that I feel comfortable with and that I have fun doing things with. But we're happy to have other people join us, and we don't feel as if we're better than everyone else. That to me is what a clique means.

When I was still in school in Livermore, there was this clique of girls in my class. I discovered that if I was with just one of those girls, we could have a good time together and we acted just like friends toward each other. But as soon as she was with other people in the clique, she just followed along with whatever they said and whatever they did, and it was as if she hadn't been friendly with me at all.

That kind of two-faced behavior is pretty hard to take, and I was quite upset by it several times. But after a while I realized that those girls weren't going to change until they didn't need their clique anymore. I tried to figure out why they wanted to be in the clique so much, and I finally decided that it's because they're basically afraid to be different. They want to be accepted by the in crowd, and they're scared that if they say something that's different from what the clique says, or if they act different, they'll be out of the group. It ends up that all the girls in a clique wear the same kind of clothes and wear their hair the same way, and if anyone inside the clique wears something different or tries a new hairstyle, they all put her down.

It sounds pretty boring to me! But when you're in school, and there's a group of girls that everyone says is really terrific and all the other girls want to be part of that group, it's natural to want to be part of it yourself. No one likes being left out of the neat stuff to do and the in parties to go to.

If you're not part of the in clique in your school, it can make you feel as if there were something wrong with you. I used to feel that I wasn't pretty enough or socially mature enough, and if I could only change those things about myself, I'd be part of the in crowd. But eventually I realized that those girls weren't superior to me in any way—they were just like everyone else. And they banded together and did everything the same way so they wouldn't be taking any chances on their own. They were probably even more scared of being laughed at or criticized than anyone else in the school!

Sometimes it's kind of hard to draw the line between being in style and doing things just because the clique does them. For instance, I don't think there's anything wrong with wearing clothes that are up-to-date and fashionable at the time you're wearing them. It may be that everyone else in the whole school is wearing the same kind of plastic bracelets or wrinkled sweatshirts or whatever the new thing is, but that's okay. I find that wearing something that's new and in often makes me feel really good and on top of things.

At the same time I don't like to feel that I *have* to wear the latest style. One day I might feel like wearing something that I've had for ages. I love it and I know it looks good on me and I feel comfortable in it. I would hate to feel that I couldn't wear my old favorite things or that if I did, I'd be kicked out of the clique and my friends wouldn't want to be seen with me.

There are lots of other parts of life that change every year—or even more often! I love learning to do the latest dance, whatever it may be, and I think it's fun to go to whatever hangout is the current in spot. But I wouldn't ever like to feel that I *had* to do these things or go to these places, and I'd be very upset if my friends made me feel that I did have to do them in order to maintain our friendship.

Those things aren't really important anyway in the long run, although sometimes it seems as if you'll die if you don't learn the latest dance. For me, though, the really important things in my life are those that I wouldn't want to change, no matter what a clique said. I feel that I have to make up my own mind about how I want to live my life, and I don't want to do things I'm not ready for or that I don't feel good about, even if every single one of my friends is doing it. That's not too likely to happen, of course, because my friends are like me in lots of ways. Still, that's how I feel about it.

PEER PRESSURE, PEER PROBLEMS

We've all heard the term *peer pressure*, and I guess that's what I'm talking about. I think it's one of the saddest things in the world to see someone doing something she really doesn't want to do, just in the hope of being accepted by the in crowd. It might be drinking or taking drugs or driving without a license or getting more involved in sex than you want to. It could be anything that a group decides is the cool thing to do that year. It's really too bad when a person gets sucked into stuff like that, without even wanting to in the first place. But it happens all the time.

I happen to feel very strongly that alcohol and drugs are very dangerous, and that teenagers shouldn't fool around with them at all. When I turned eighteen on *The Love Boat*—I guess I should say that it was Vicki's eighteenth birthday show—the story dealt with the problems and dangers of alcoholism. I thought that show had a very important message, and I was really glad that the writers had come up with the idea.

One reason I felt good about it was that I think my character, Vicki Stubing, often has an effect on people who watch the show. A lot of people like Vicki, and without wanting to sound conceited, I think a lot of kids may try to be like her. I take this seriously, and I don't like to do anything on the show that wouldn't be appropriate for the kids who may be watching.

The way I got into Mrs. Reagan's Action program, which is designed to help children and young people stay away from drugs, was kind of interesting. It was because there was a script for a *Love Boat* show in which Vicki tried drugs. Well, I thought the idea was terrible, and I refused to do the show. It was the first time I had ever made a fuss about a script in any way, and I think everyone was kind of surprised. But I just couldn't do it. For one thing, the way the story was written, Vicki's dad never talked to her about the drug thing until the very end, and then what he said was something like, "I'm glad this happened, because it's brought us closer together."

Well, really! What kind of a parent would say, "I'm glad you tried drugs" to his daughter? I thought it was awful.

But the main reason I didn't want to do the show was that I felt it just wasn't true to Vicki's character. I felt as if I know Vicki pretty well. I thought that I personally would never try drugs on a whim, and neither would Vicki. It just didn't feel right to me. And I felt, too, that the character I play on TV was a role model for kids who were watching, and if they saw Vicki trying drugs, it could open the door for them. They might say to themselves, "Well, if Vicki tried it, it can't be so bad. I'll try it too." And I didn't want to do that.

Anyway, it was the first time I'd ever taken a stand like that at work. I guess it was the first time it had ever come up in a work situation. Thank goodness, Gavin MacLeod, who plays my father, Captain Stubing, agreed and supported me—he even held my hand at the meeting in which we discussed it. The next thing I knew, someone had told someone in Washington, D.C., about it, and that person knew Mrs. Reagan or knew about the program. So I got a call asking me if I wanted to be involved in Mrs. Reagan's Action program. Of course, I did. And Gavin joined me!

It's been really interesting. I go around and give seminars at schools and colleges, and I talk to the kids about my personal feelings about drugs and alcohol. I've spoken at rallies on college campuses and at assemblies at lots of high schools and junior highs. And I've given a course in drug awareness a few times, usually for younger kids.

I took a course at University of Southern California so I would know how to talk to the younger kids. The idea is to make them aware of what drugs really are. Often the whole topic of drugs is shrouded in mystery, so it's made into a really scary thing. Well, that's kind of exciting to kids, along with its being scary. What I try to do is explain in very down-to-earth terms what drugs are and what they do to you. I try to take away the mystery—and the monsters—so the children don't feel that *drugs* is a bad word that they shouldn't use. Then after I explain what the different kinds of drugs are, I work with them on how to say no to drugs. We do role playing. I have them do a skit in which one child is offering drugs to the others, and the others have to say no. One important thing we work on is body language. If you're feeling scared or uncomfortable when someone is trying to get you to try drugs, it shows in the way you speak and the way you hold your body. So we work on developing a kind of body language that lets the other person know you really mean it when you say no.

I taught one of these courses for the younger grades at the school I went to in Los Angeles, and I felt really good about it. I felt that I was contributing something important to these kids, who are going to be exposed to drugs one way or another during their teen years.

I like doing this kind of course with younger kids, but I enjoy the assemblies with older kids too. I don't have a set speech that I give. Usually I'm not the first speaker, so while I listen to the introductory speech I have a chance to watch the audience and see how they're reacting, and that gives me some ideas about what I should say. Each audience is a little different, and if I gave them all the same speech, I think it wouldn't be as good.

To me drug prevention is much better than drug rehabilitation. It's so much better to stop it before it starts than to try to get people off drugs after they're hooked. I've visited rehabilitation centers for teenagers, and it's just terrible to see kids my own age or younger who have just about destroyed themselves.

I never really wanted to try drugs myself. It's not that I think it's a sin; it's more a feeling that I don't need it at all. I try to explain that to other kids. I've seen what it can do to people and I try to tell them what a waste it is—it's a waste of money, of course, but more important, it's a waste of a person's life. It takes away all the good things a person has been given to live a valuable life with. And I try to help other kids realize that they don't need drugs either.

I'm not sure why this was never a problem for me. I guess in a way I was just lucky. But I think it helps to practice saying no. It may sound kind of silly, but if you practice in a role-playing situation, it's much easier to do it in real life when it comes up. It's like knowing your lines for a play.

Also it helped that my friends weren't into drugs. Of course, there are a lot of people in Los Angeles on all kinds of drugs, and some of them are pretty tragic cases. But the kids I know well don't do that stuff, so I was never subjected to pressure from my friends to "try it just once" or whatever it is people say. I'm happy about that because I don't want to try drugs myself and because I don't ever want to see my friends or anyone I care about get started on that dangerous path.

FRIENDS FOREVER?

Remember when you were little and you said to your friend, "We'll be best friends forever and ever"? Or maybe you made secret promises in a code language that no one else could read, saying that you'd be best friends until death.

I did stuff like that. And now that I'm a little older, I still feel that way about my friends, even though I don't sign a secret pact in blood anymore!

My friends are really important to me—they're part of my life. Some of them are the girls I had over for slumber parties while I was in school, and I still remember how much fun we had playing Sardines and all those crazy games. Others are people I've met since I started working in Los Angeles. Last New Year's Eve a bunch of us got together at one guy's house, and we played charades and listened to old music and reminisced. After midnight we ended up talking about what we wanted for the new year, and everybody really opened up. One guy said he really hoped he'd be able to have a serious relationship with a girl—he hadn't had one before, but now he felt like he was ready for it. It was so nice that we all trusted one another enough to say things like that.

I'm sure I'll make new friends in every new stage of my life—at least I hope so. But I feel that I'll always care about the friends I have now. They know so much about me, and we've been through so much together as children and as teenagers. No one I meet later will have all that shared experience. I don't want to lose that. So I plan to stay friends with these special people for the rest of my life.

Dear Jill,

I have a problem with my friend. She's really a great person, but recently I found out that she's been stealing things from stores. They're not big things, and I don't think she does it very often, but it makes me very nervous and upset. I don't know if I should say anything to her about it or not. I'm not sure if she knows I'm aware of it. What should I do about this problem? Please help.

Anne S.

Dear Anne,

It's always difficult when a friend does something that you know is wrong. You feel torn between the friendship and your own moral values. And you're probably worried that someone will find out, and your friend will be hauled off to jail!

When a good friend does something like this, I think you have to talk to her about it, or it will spoil your friendship. Maybe you could tell her it makes you uncomfortable. After all, she's infringing on your peace of mind. There's nothing wrong with being honest with her about it. Try saying, "I really like you and I want to be your friend. But it makes it hard for me when I know you're doing something wrong. It's up to you to do something about it—I can't control what you do. But I'd have an easier time if you didn't do it.'' You don't have to be overbearing or moralistic about it, but maybe hearing how you feel will give her a chance to see it from a different perspective.

On the other hand it may be that you've gotten caught up in a crowd that thinks shoplifting, or other kinds of illegal behavior, is cool. In that case, the only thing to do is stay away from them. It's unlikely that you'll be able to change their feelings about it right now, although it may be just a phase they're going through, and by next year they'll have outgrown this kind of childish rebellion. You have a right to your own values, and even if other people make fun of them, you'll have more respect for yourself if you stick to them.

Dear Jill,

I've been friends with this one girl for a long time—since we were in kindergarten together. She's a really nice, smart person and I like her a lot. But lately I've noticed that she doesn't take very good care of herself. In fact, she's a slob. She's overweight, and her hair looks stringy and dirty, and she doesn't bother to dress nicely at all. I feel bad about it, but I don't know what to say to her. I think if I say anything, she might feel insulted. Is there anything I can do about this?

Marilyn W.

Dear Marilyn,

I know how you feel. It makes you unhappy to see your friend let herself become such a mess. And you probably can't help feeling that, when you're seen with someone like her, it reflects on you—it cuts out on your action!

Don't imagine that you're being selfish to feel that way. It's only natural. You're ready to have the boys notice you, and you're afraid they'll lump you in with your less-than-attractive friend.

I think it's great that you're concerned about your

friend instead of just being worried about yourself. But it may be that your friend is feeling terrified about growing up and getting into the social swing of boyfriends and dating. By letting herself get fat and by not bothering to try to look her best, she may be setting up a convenient excuse for herself for why she's not the most popular girl in town.

If that's the problem, you won't be able to solve it. But if you feel your friend will be receptive to a little help, here are some things you can try.

For a weight problem you could say, "Gosh, I'm getting a little too fat. I need to go on a diet but it's hard to do it all by myself. I need some encouragement. Will you do it with me? Then at least when we go somewhere, there'll be two of us that aren't eating!" By putting the problem on yourself, you make her feel she's helping you out, and that might make it easier for her to do something about her weight.

If you think she needs help with her clothes, you might ask if she wants to go shopping with you. Then when you're both looking around at the stuff on the racks, you can steer her toward something you think would look good on her. It might be an outfit or just a color you think would suit her. It may be that she feels intimidated by salespeople or just by the whole idea of shopping for clothes. And when you say something looks nice on her, it might be the incentive she needs.

Another way you could help is by clipping out pictures from magazines of clothes or makeup or hairstyles you think would be good for her. You can say, "I saw this picture, and I thought it was really flattering for this girl. I bet it would look great on you."

The thing is, if she tries something new and she gets complimented on it, it will encourage her to keep on caring about how she looks.

Dear Jill,

I was best friends with Amy for a really long time. But now she's sort of dropped me and she's best friends with another girl. I wish I could be friends with Amy again. Should I tell her how I feel?

Cynthia K.

Dear Cynthia,

First of all, don't do anything mean. You'll probably be sorry for it later. And it won't help your problem. Everyone feels hurt when a friend deserts them—it's really hard. But you have to realize that it's not your fault. Sometimes your friend may just feel that she's growing away from you, and she doesn't even know why. Or she may feel that the two of you are too close, and she doesn't have a chance to get to know other people—she needs to reach out and have new experiences. A "best friend" relationship can sometimes get to be too suffocating for both of you, and as you get older you may need to branch out a little bit.

There's not a whole lot you can do about your immediate problem. A heart-to-heart talk with your former best friend isn't going to do any good, and it will end up making you feel like a fool. It's much better to find other friends to spend time with now, rather than wallowing in your own misery. Of course, since misery loves company, you have to be careful to find the right kind of friends. It's not a good idea to hang around with a couple of other girls who are feeling left out and sorry for themselves. But I'm sure you have plenty of other friends you can get closer to and do things with, and that will take your mind off your disappointment.

Bear in mind, though, that Amy may just be feeling a need to try out new friendships. In a little while she may find that she misses you as much as you miss her, and she may want to be your best friend again. If that happens, you have to decide whether to be a good friend yourself and to be there when she needs you. Loyalty is an important part of friendship, but remember that you and your friends are changing and testing new experiences and relationships as you're growing up. If Amy wants to be best friends again, it will be up to you to decide whether you'll feel comfortable with that or not. If you will, that's fine. If you won't, don't feel too bad—you'll find other friends to share your hopes and secrets with.

Chapter 5

The Dating Game

I DON'T KNOW about you, but I seem to think about boys a lot. When I was much younger, I didn't really think about them one way or the other. I might have been friends with a certain boy or I might not, but it didn't make too much difference either way. But then you get to a certain point in your life, and whammo! It seems as if you've never seen a boy before! All of a sudden you start looking at them in a whole new way and wondering if the boy you like will ever like you—and you don't just want him to like you as a friend either!

But really, even though I think about boys just like any other teenager, I haven't dated all that much. People are sometimes surprised when I say this, because they think that anyone who's on TV leads this really glamorous life with dates and dancing every night. Maybe some people do lead this kind of life, but I never have!

It's not that I'm a total recluse, of course, but it really is true that I haven't been out with very many boys. And it wasn't because I didn't want to—it was because I didn't get asked very often!

Actually, though, it wasn't so terrible. For one thing, none of my close girlfriends had steady boyfriends until our senior year in high school, so I wasn't the only one without a date every Saturday night. We'd get together and go to movies and stuff and have a really good time.

GOING OUT IN GROUPS

Besides going to movies or going out to eat, I went to a lot of dances with a group of my friends if none of us had a date. We called it "going stag," and I usually didn't mind it at all. I'd dance with the guys that had also come without dates, or my girlfriends and I would dance together. That way we could laugh at each other when we messed up trying out the latest dances!

When I think about it now, it seems to me that we had just as much fun going stag as the other kids who had dates did. In some ways going out with a group of friends is actually more fun than going with a date, because you don't have any pressure to do anything except just be yourself and have fun. You're not worrying all the time about what your date thinks of you or if he really likes you or if you're acting like an idiot or something. When you're with a group of your friends, you can just goof off and no one will think anything about it.

But when I was still in school, there were times when I went to a dance without a date and I felt bad about it. I'd think, *Why can't I have a date?* and I'd wonder if there was something the matter with me. I felt as if there must be a reason why I didn't have dates and other girls did.

There probably was a reason, but it wasn't the kind of reason I thought it was. I was always worrying that I wasn't pretty enough or smart enough or fun enough to be with or something. But I don't believe it was anything like that. I think the reason I didn't date a whole lot was that with everything else that was going on in my life and with all my energy being taken up with school and work all week long, I just wasn't really ready to date.

That may sound weird, but I think it's true. And there's nothing wrong with that. People grow up physically at different rates, so why wouldn't they grow up socially at different rates too? But I have to admit that it helped that none of my close friends were dating much either!

"I'VE GOT TO HAVE A BOYFRIEND!"

Have you ever said something like that? I have—I bet everyone has! Sometimes it seems as if everyone in the whole world except you has a wonderful boyfriend who's madly in love with them, and you're the only teenage girl in the entire United States who has nothing to do but sit home on Saturday night and watch reruns. (Actually I hope you watch *The Love Boat* if you are home on Saturday nights!)

Of course, in your saner moments you know that isn't really true. Still, I think everyone feels like this sometimes. It might be that your best friends, or several of your friends, do have boyfriends, and you feel as if you'd like to try this exciting new experience too. I can remember when I was in junior high, I used to pray every night, "Please make me beautiful and make Johnny—or whoever it was—like me." I felt as if I just had to have a boyfriend right then.

Maybe that feeling is just a normal part of being a teenager. But guess what? It doesn't necessarily go away as you get older. I'm not sure if that's good news or bad news! There are times when I'm sitting around on the set with my friends—all of them are older than I am—and all of them are saying, "I need to find a boyfriend." Maybe they've just broken up with somebody, but all of them are saying the same thing my friends at school used to say—and I'm joining right in.

The only time I can think of when I didn't say that was right after I broke up with someone. At that point I felt that the last thing in the world I wanted was to get involved again! But most of the time we're all moaning about exactly the same thing. Sometimes I just have to mentally step back and laugh at the whole bunch of us. But then again, let's face it—a relationship between a guy and a girl can be pretty exciting and wonderful. Why shouldn't we all want it to happen to us?

It's interesting to hang around and talk things over with my older friends, and I often feel that I get a different slant on things than I would get from friends my own age. But sometimes it gets a little heavy too. I remember one time when we were sitting around on the set and one of my friends was talking about a date she was going to have that night. She was saying she didn't know whether she should take him home to her apartment afterward to spend the night.

That's a whole different ball game as far as I'm concerned. I don't know how I'll feel when I'm older, but right now that's definitely not for me. And sometimes it makes me feel a little uncomfortable even to talk about it. So when she told us that, I just said, "O-kay! I'll catch you later."

I think it's important to figure out where you are for yourself. You're the only person who can know what you're ready for and what you're not ready for. And only you can know where to draw the line for yourself. I can sit around with a bunch of people who are older than I am and we can talk about how we all want to find a boyfriend. But I'm not ready to talk about taking some guy home with me, even if that's what everyone else in the group has in mind. They have to decide what they want for themselves, and I have a responsibility to make decisions for myself too. I don't want to rush into something I'm really not feeling right about just because other people are doing it.

IS HE A HEARTBREAKER OR A NERD?

One thing that just about all of us have gone through is the experience where there's two really terrific guys in the school, and every single girl in every class is madly in love with them. These guys are Mr. Personality or Mr. Gorgeous or Mr. All-Around Successful-at-Everything-He-Tries. So there you are, wishing that he'd give you a smile, and knowing that every other girl is wishing the same thing.

It seems that everyone I've ever talked to has been

through this, so it must happen all the time. It's really hard, especially when you try all the tricks you read in magazines about asking him to help you with math or talking to him about his favorite sport, and then he turns around and asks someone else for a date. The only good thing you can say about it is that you're not the only girl who's going to feel crushed when he doesn't choose her. (But that doesn't really do anybody much good.)

It seems to me that the best thing to do in that situation is to stop trying to snare the guy that everyone is crazy about and find someone else who's a little bit more available. After all, when you stop to think about it, it's really not possible that there are only two guys who are nice and attractive and all those other good things. There must be others—if you just take time to stop and look!

Of course, it can be hard to give up your dream guy, even when you know that's exactly what he is—a dream that isn't ever going to become a reality. Sometimes it can feel a lot safer to make up fantasies about some guy who you know is never going to look your way or ask you out. That way you don't have to deal with the realities, like: what would you say if he *did* ask you out? What would you wear on a date with him? Would your mom even let you go out with him if he asked you?

Another thing that sometimes makes it hard to set your sights on another guy—maybe one you haven't ever thought about going out with—is the same kind of peer pressure that we all feel in different aspects of our lives. I can remember when I was in school in Livermore and there was a whole group of girls that were kind of the in crowd, and they all liked this one boy. One day I was talking to some of those girls and I said, "Oh, I think Billy is so cute." Well, Billy wasn't the boy they had decided was so neat, so they all looked at me and went, "Billy? Oh, yuck!"

I didn't really care much about Billy one way or the other—Billy isn't his real name, by the way!—although I did think he was cute. But what if I *had* really liked him? I might have felt so put down by their reaction to what I said that I would have changed my mind. Or I might have just *said* I'd changed my mind, which would really be the same thing in the end. It might have been more important to me to be part of the in crowd of girls in the school than to get to know a boy I thought was cute-looking.

When I think about it, I realize that it's really stupid to let other people make your decisions for you and dictate who you like and what you do. I mean, maybe the other girls were right, and Billy was basically a nerd even though he was cute. But how would I ever have known for sure if I'd let myself go along with them?

Sometimes it's awfully hard to stand up for your own ideas or feelings. But there's no rule that says other people are right more often than you are. And if you let yourself go along with the crowd all the time, you might miss out on meeting the true love of your life!

Besides, look at it this way: If you set your sights on a boy that no one else is interested in at that very moment, you've got a pretty good chance of getting to know him and going out with him at least enough times to decide if you really like him. Whereas if you keep trying to get Mr. Popular to notice you, even when he does, you're going to have to fight off all that competition from the other girls all the time. It's kind of a strain on the relationship. My attitude is, look for the guy whose wonderful qualities haven't been noticed by anyone else. He's probably a great person, and you'll end up with a date for the Halloween Dance while all the other girls are scheming to see who goes out with the one guy they all want. Who's better off? Think about it!

DON'T PUT YOURSELF DOWN!

Do you sometimes catch yourself thinking things like, "Oh, I'm not pretty enough for a guy like him," or "The neat guy I like will never notice me—I can't ever think of anything interesting to say to him." I've found myself thinking stuff like that many times, especially when I was younger. I think everybody does it. But that doesn't mean it's a good idea!

And comparing yourself with another person doesn't make much sense either, because each person is completely unique from everyone else. Some other girl may be gorgeous to look at, but she may be a total dimwit in class. There are boys who seem to think great looks are all that matters, but there are lots of other boys who would rather be able to talk to a girl than just gaze at her beautiful face. After all, how long can anyone do that?

But there are times when you feel as if there's nothing right about you—not your looks, not your brains, not your personality, *nothing*! It's not true, and really deep down you know that, but sometimes it's hard to remember!

Working on a television series, I've had a chance to work with a lot of really handsome guys, and some of them are supernice as well! It might be someone like Christopher Knight—*The Brady Bunch* was my favorite show ever when I was little, and I thought if I could meet Christopher Knight in person, I'd just die! And I was crazy about Willie Ames and Grant Goodeve when I used to watch *Eight Is Enough*, so you can imagine how I felt when they appeared as guest stars on *The Love Boat*.

It's hard when some truly fabulous guy is on our show, or when I do a guest appearance on another show like *Fantasy Island* or *Trapper John, M.D.* Sometimes I can't even concentrate on what I'm supposed to be doing, because I'm just staring at this really neat guy and wishing he would ask me out. And all the time I'm worried that I'm not pretty enough or smart enough or whatever enough, and I'm thinking that of course, he won't be interested in me. Usually it turns out that these terrific guys already have girlfriends, so I never find out for sure if they would have asked me out or not. But still, the next time it happens, I start worrying all over again.

I bet if you asked any girl you know, even the most popular one in school, you'd find out that everybody has these thoughts. Everybody worries that they won't be good enough in some way, and the boys they like won't be interested in them. I don't really know how to stop worrying about this—I still do it myself! But at least you can realize with one part of your mind that it doesn't have anything to do with reality.

The problem is your own image of yourself, which probably is nothing like what other people really think of you! So I guess the best thing to do is to tell yourself that other people do like you—you have friends who think you're great. And they probably have a more objective view of you than you do yourself, so why not take their word for it that you're a wonderful person?

FIRST LOVE

It's really exciting when you have a boyfriend for the first time. For a while it seems as if you can't think about anything else, and you may feel absolutely certain that this is the love of your life, and there will never be anyone else for you.

Sometimes that turns out to be true—there are people who get married to the first boy they went out with in the seventh grade—but I don't think it happens very often. And I think that's really a good thing. It's much more fun to get to know a lot of different guys, and it helps you find out what you like and don't like in a boy-girl relationship. Of course, when you're in love for the first time, you don't want to think that it won't last forever. But remember, if it doesn't, you're definitely not the only one it's happened to!

When I was in junior high, there was this boy who was a year ahead of me, and I thought he was just the neatest guy in the whole world. I liked him for an entire year, and then finally he got interested in me. I was so happy! So we started going out, and we were going together for one big month. And then I found out he was cheating on me! It was terrible. I was so upset and so mad at him. First I thought about telling him, "You have to choose—her or me." But then I realized that even if he chose me, I wouldn't trust him anymore, and I'd never feel the same about him again.

So I broke up with him. When we were going steady, he had given me this green plastic glow-in-the-dark thing from Magic Mountain amusement park, and I wore it on a chain around my neck all the time. I never took it off. But when we broke up, I threw it away—I wasn't going to give it back to him!

Now I think he was a total jerk, and I can't understand what I ever saw in him in the first place. But I guess that's just because I'm older now. My ideas and my feelings about people have changed, and the people I like and respect now are different in lots of ways from the people I liked when I was younger. So for me, it's a good thing I didn't marry the first guy I fell in love with!

IS THERE A NICE WAY TO SAY NO?

Saying no—turning down a date—is one of the hardest things in the world to do, I think. I'm always worried that I'll hurt the guy's feelings, so I make excuses. At the roller rink, if some guy that I didn't like much asked me to skate, I'd always say, "Oh, not now. My ankle hurts and I have to sit down for a while." I guess he got the message when he saw me skating with someone else two minutes later!

Actually I'm not sure if making this kind of excuse is the best way to handle things. Sometimes I think I'm trying not to hurt a guy's feelings—but other times I think I'm just chickening out. Maybe it would be better to make it clear to a guy that you really don't want to go out with him. It's not that you have to go to your cousin's wedding or your grandmother's seventieth birthday party; it's that you don't want to date him at all.

In one way, of course, it would be better to do this. For one thing he wouldn't keep calling you, and you wouldn't have to think up more and more excuses until he finally got the message. On the other hand it seems to me that whatever you say about this, his feelings *will* be hurt.

Maybe the best way to handle it is to tell him that you appreciate his asking you out, but you just don't think of him as a person to date. You can go on to say that you like him as a friend—if that's true!—and you hope you can stay friends with him. Then I guess it's up to him to decide to be friends or not.

It's great if things work out this way, because it's always nice to have a boy for a friend, and also you never know how your feelings toward him might change as time goes on. Later on you might want to date him after all. But I think it's hard to do this. I think that however much you talk about being friends and wrap it up, a guy's feelings will be hurt when he asks you for a date and you tell him you don't think of him in that way. If he's a pretty together person, he might not be too upset, and you can have a good time being friends with him. But lots of guys would feel embarrassed or humiliated by this, no matter how nicely you say it.

Still, if you feel sure that you're never going to want to go out with this boy in the near future, no matter how often he asks you, it's probably better to tell him that right away and not let it drag on with more and more phone calls. There isn't any point in letting someone like that think that you'd be happy to go out with him if only you didn't have important family engagements that you can't get out of for the next twelve months! You might as well get it over with and save both of you some embarrassing moments.

HOW TO ASK A BOY OUT

I hope you don't think I'm going to give you some wonderful advice on the best way to ask boys out, because I think it's really hard to do! I get very nervous about it, even though I believe that there's no reason at all why a girl can't ask a boy out instead of waiting for a boy to ask her.

Actually I'm pretty lucky, because when I go to parties and other social events that are mainly for my work, I often ask another actor or someone from the show to go with me. And we both know it's business, so it's easier than just asking a guy for a regular date, but still it's given me some practice in how to do it.

But it's especially hard for me to ask out a boy I really like. I guess the reason's pretty obvious—I mean, if it's someone you don't care that much about, then you won't be bothered if he says no. But when it's a guy I like, I start worrying about what to do if he turns me down. What will I say if he gives me some dumb excuse, like his grandmother died—and I know it's the fourth time this month that she's died?

When I think about it, I guess my feelings about being turned down by a guy I like should give me an idea of how a boy feels when I say no to him. And if I'm annoyed or humiliated when a guy gives me a stupid excuse instead of just telling me he's not interested, I guess he would feel the same way if I gave him some flimsy made-up excuse for why I'm not going out with him. Boys probably aren't that much different from girls, although sometimes it seems as if they're from another planet!

WHAT DO BOYS THINK ABOUT GIRLS?

I used to wonder about this all the time—in fact, I still do! You'd think that having an older brother would help. It would be nice if older brothers or even younger brothers would give the girls some insight into how boys' minds work. But I guess they hardly ever do. And even when my brother told me stories about his social life, most of the time they weren't very helpful.

I do remember one story, though, that made a big impression on me. It was when Chuck was in high school and he really thought he was Mr. Cool. He was dating this girl who was very pretty, and he really liked her a lot. But one time they were at a big dance at school, and he found out that she was telling put-down stories about him in the ladies' room. I think his friends' girlfriends told him about it, and so did some of his friends who were girls—he always had both boys and girls as friends.

Anyway, he felt like a fool. Of course, that was the end of their relationship, but it really made him feel bad. He felt as if she'd been making a fool of him all along.

When he told me about it, it sounded so familiar. It was just like when my own girlfriends told me about boys who talked about them to other boys or who did other things that made my friends feel they'd been put down. It made me think that boys aren't so different from us after all. They get nervous about asking a girl out, and they worry about whether or not the girls will think they're attractive and smart and all that stuff. It's just the same thing we worry about, only in reverse.

It's funny though. Even after hearing a story like that, I still thought of boys as a mysterious kind of creature that I didn't understand at all. I was always wondering what they thought or how they felt. It's like another side of people that's always in the shadows, and I can't get a clear view of it. And even though I can stop and say to myself, "Don't be silly, boys are just as nervous and worried as you are," it doesn't always stay with me, and I don't always remember it when it would be most helpful. But I try!

TALKING A DIFFERENT LANGUAGE

Do you sometimes feel when you're with a boy that the two of you are like creatures from two different planets? You're both trying to get through to each other, but for some reason the communication system isn't working.

I think this sometimes happens when the two of you have different ideas of what you expect, from the date or from the whole relationship. You may have started from two different basic assumptions, and when that happens, it's pretty hard to communicate in a way that the other person will understand.

For example, if you've been going out every Friday and Saturday evening with the same guy for a few months, you probably aren't going out with anyone else. For one thing, you don't have time. So you probably assume that the two of you are going together, and that he isn't seeing anyone else either. So you will feel very hurt and betrayed if you discover that he's spending every Sunday and Wednesday evening with another girl.

But your boyfriend may not even understand what you're upset about. He thinks that because the two of you never actually said you wouldn't date other people, you were both free to do so. He'll tell you you could have gone out with another guy, and he wouldn't have been upset! (But, you say, you *know* my parents don't let me date on any nights but weekends—how could I have gone out with someone else?)

Then he'll say that you shouldn't be upset, that of course, he likes you best—isn't that why he spends his weekend evenings with you and nobody else? But since you aren't free to go out on other nights, he doesn't see why you should mind if at those times he sees another girl.

So there you are. You can't think of anything to say to him that will really make him understand why you're in tears about this, and you can't think of a good answer to his oh-so-reasonable attitudes. Even though you know he's all wrong, you can't put your finger on exactly *why* he's wrong.

This kind of thing happens all the time. Maybe it's because in spite of the changes in our society and the changes in what women are allowed to do and expected to do, boys and girls are still brought up differently in lots of ways. I think that, as hard as it is to believe, lots of times the boys really *don't* understand what the girls are trying to tell them. And it's even harder to explain what the problem is when you're already upset and angry.

Probably the best thing to do is to try to work things out from the beginning so both of you understand what the ground rules of your relationship are. Explaining your point of view or your deeply held feelings is a lot easier when you're both calmly sitting in a booth over a Coke or walking home from the library. But at those times it seems as if nothing will ever come between you, and it's hard to think of the things that might need to be talked out and explained! Still, it's worth trying to solve some of those common problems—like are you going steady or not, and if you are, what does that mean?—before they get too big and out of control.

The communication problem isn't always between you and the boy you're going steady with though. I can remember a date I had a few years ago that didn't work out at all. It seemed as if the guy expected something different from me than what I was doing, and I guess I expected something different from him. And we weren't communicating even about the little things! I thought we were going out to eat somewhere fancy, so I got fairly dressed up, and then it turned out that we were going to some little diner. It's not that I mind going to a diner—and this one was kind of fun—but I was really overdressed, and I felt uncomfortable. Then afterward it seemed that everything he suggested doing was either too far away or would keep me out too late, and everything I suggested was something he hated or a movie or whatever that he'd already seen. We couldn't find anything we both wanted to do! So finally he took me home at some ridiculously early time and said good night.

I was so relieved to get inside and close the door! And I bet he was relieved that our date was over too. To this day I'm not exactly sure what the problem was. Maybe I just wasn't ready at that time to go out on a date with someone I didn't already know pretty well. Or maybe he and I weren't the same kind of people at all, and we never would have gotten along very well even if we'd tried. I really don't know. But I think it's too bad that we couldn't explain to each other what the problem was. If we'd been able to communicate a little better with each other, I think maybe we could have had a fun evening! Ever since then, I've made much more of an effort to explain my point of view, and I've tried to make sure that the guy I'm with understands what I'm saying. It's not always so easy, but when it works, it makes things a lot more relaxed.

BREAKING UP IS HARD TO DO!

Isn't that really true? Everyone knows it is—in fact, it's even the title of a song, that's how universal the feeling is. Somehow it's just never easy to tell a guy that you're through as far as your relationship is concerned. There are lots of things involved: You don't want to hurt his feelings and you're afraid he'll be angry or—even worse—really upset and sad. Also sometimes you feel that even though you don't want to go out with him anymore, at least he's one guy that wants to date you! What if you break up with him and then nobody else asks you out?

I think we all have those thoughts, even when we know in the logical part of our brain that they don't actually make much sense. And especially when you first start dating, you feel so unsure of yourself, you sometimes catch yourself feeling grateful to the guy that asks you out! That's really dumb, isn't it? But we all do it from time to time.

All these things get in the way when you decide it's

time to break up. And even though you can say to yourself, "Okay, now, I'm just going to be very calm and I'm not going to get mad or upset or emotional or crazy and I'm not going to let him change my mind or talk me into not breaking up"—you can say all those things and then when the time comes, your hands get all clammy and you're stammering and babbling and not saying any of the things you had all planned out in your mind.

Of course, sometimes the problem is that you don't know exactly why you want to break up with him. I broke up with a guy a couple of years ago, and I really didn't know what was wrong. Maybe he was getting too serious about our relationship and that wasn't what I was ready for at the time. Or maybe I was just getting kind of tired of him. I'm not sure what the problem was. I just know that I didn't want to be with him anymore. And I got myself really worked up about it.

What happened was that I was going on a cruise for *The Love Boat* and our last stop was Amsterdam. So my boyfriend—I'll call him Cal—was going to be traveling in Europe with some friends, and he decided to come and meet me in Amsterdam. We had this all planned before I decided to break up with him—we worked it out a long time in advance. But then I realized that I didn't want to go out with him anymore. And I was just dreading the end of the cruise and meeting him in Amsterdam—I could hardly think about anything else.

It's kind of silly when I think about it. After all, if I decide I don't want to see someone, it's my right to make that decision, and there really isn't any reason to get nervous about it. But that's what I did. And it was while I was on that cruise that I gained so much weight, and that's something I definitely didn't need to do. But I think I was scared that I was getting in too deep with this relationship and at the same time I was scared of breaking it off. So to take my mind off the whole thing I just kept on eating!

You might have already figured out that I didn't have a great time in Amsterdam, even though I tried to see as little of Cal as I could. When I did see him, I was tense, and I know I was acting weird. But he never said a word about it.

Finally, after I got home from that trip, I knew that I had to do something about the problem. I was still really scared to do it, but I felt that it wasn't fair to Cal to keep seeing him when I didn't want to and I didn't feel the way I had before about him. And I couldn't lie and say I did want to see him either. I knew it was really going to be hard to do, but I felt I owed it to him to be honest.

It would be nice if there were some way that you could get someone else to do these unpleasant things for you, or if there were some wise person who could tell you exactly how to handle it with the least amount of pain. But I guess you pretty much have to work it out for yourself. I talked to my friend Nicky about it, and I was saying, "Oh, my gosh, what am I going to do? What am I going to say?" and all those things everyone says.

Here's what Nicky said: "Just tell him it's over, Jill. That's all you have to do."

In a way she was right, but it wasn't very helpful to me to hear that! I said, "Sure, that's easy to say, but I don't see you doing that with no problems!"

That's really the point. It's easy for someone to tell you what you should say and do, and it's easy to understand that they're right. But it's a whole lot harder to actually do it and to say those things. And for me it was really hard, because I'd never done it before.

But no matter how difficult it is, you just have to gather up your courage and do it and get it over with. And when you do, you feel so much better. After I broke up with Cal, I felt such a relief. It was like a load off my back. I felt that at last I could get back to my normal life without worrying about what I was going to do about Cal all the time.

But it's funny. I think he must have realized that it was coming. I found out later that he had gone around saying to people that *he* was going to break up with *me*, and this was before he met me in Amsterdam! It seemed really strange to me that he would do that, but later on I thought that maybe he wanted other people to believe that he was the one to do the breaking up instead of me. Sometimes guys feel that having someone break up with them is an insult, and it hurts their pride even more than it hurts their feelings. (Some girls are like this too!)

But when I found out that Cal had said that to people I knew, I lost a lot of respect for him. I think it's pretty pathetic to be that worried about your pride and about what other people might think of you. The breaking up was between Cal and me, and as far as I was concerned, other people's opinions had nothing to do with it. After that I was glad that I'd said good-bye to him, and I didn't worry anymore about how hurt he might have been!

I think when you decide to break up with a guy, you have to try to do it in the way that will hurt him the least. I tried to think about how I'd want someone to tell me the bad news—you know, I'd want them to be honest but not mean or nasty. So I tried to do that with Cal. The other thing is that I think it's better to do it face to face, even though it's a lot harder that way. It seems as if you're hiding if you write a letter or even if you call the guy on the phone. I guess if you really can't do it, then you can't. But for myself, I feel better about it and I feel it's more final if I do it in person.

AFTER YOU BREAK UP, THEN WHAT?

There are always other guys out there. I know that's what everybody always tells you, but it's really true!

Sometimes, especially if you've been going with one guy for a long time, it takes a while to open your eyes and look around and see who else is out there who would be fun to get to know. You've temporarily forgotten that there are other attractive and interesting guys whom you're now free to flirt with.

Another problem is that after you've ended a steady relationship with a boy, you may not be ready to jump into another one. When I broke up with Cal, I felt as if I just wanted to stay away from guys for a while. The end of it had been very hard, and it had made me so nervous that I didn't want to get involved again right away. And if your steady boyfriend broke up with you, instead of you breaking up with him, you might be feeling so hurt that all you want to do is crawl into a hole and never look at another boy again. I've felt that way sometimes. But luckily it doesn't last forever.

After a while, when you start wanting to get out in the swim of things again, there's likely to be another boy who turns out to be even nicer and more exciting than the guy you went out with before. Sometimes it might be someone you thought was kind of a nerd last time you looked at him—but that was three years ago and wow, has he changed! The thing to remember is, you just never know.

There's this really neat guy on another show—I won't tell you his name or which show he's on, because I don't know if he likes me. But I think he's great. And the weird thing is, he never dated in high school. I was so surprised to find that out! I don't know if he was one of those geeks or nerds—although it's pretty hard to believe that he could ever have been like that! He says he was always tripping and falling over his feet, and he was totally tongue-tied around girls. When he described it, I knew just what he meant and I'm sure you know guys like that too.

Now he's really gorgeous. But he recently told a mutual friend that he still has a hard time asking a girl out. I can't understand why! But I hope he'll get over that problem with me—I'll let you know how things work out!

Dear Jill,

There's this really terrific boy who goes to my school. The good news is that he doesn't have a girlfriend, but the bad news is that he doesn't seem to know that I exist! I'd really like to get to know him better so hopefully he would ask me out. But I don't know how to get started. I can't just walk up and say, "Hi, let's talk." How can I get him to notice me?

Joan D.

Dear Joan,

You don't say in your letter whether this boy is in any of your classes. If he is, of course, you have a ready-made opportunity to start up a conversation—about the homework assignment or how tough the teacher is or something like that. This is a tried-and-true method, and the good thing about it is that your motives don't seem so obvious.

If he's not in your classes, maybe there's an afterschool club he belongs to that you could join. This gives you an interest in common that can be an easy way to get to know him. Just remember, though, that if it's a scuba-diving club and you're scared of the water, it's probably not going to work out!

Another idea is to do something to catch his attention—nothing too weird, just something that will make him turn his head and notice you. For example, one time this really cute guy was on the tennis court across from mine—he was really incredible-looking! So I started teaching my friend karate, just to make him wonder what we were doing. He made a kidding comment like, "Hey, come on, no violence on the court!" And there we were, talking and having a good time. I don't know if this always works, but give it a try!

Dear Jill,

I have a terrible problem. There's a boy who just won't leave me alone, and I can't stand him! He's a total nerd, but he asks me out all the time. He hangs around after school waiting for me and he walks home with me, even though I try to avoid him. I always say no when he asks me for a date, but it doesn't discourage him. What can I do to get this guy out of my life?

Michelle P.

Dear Michelle,

Obviously, this guy is infringing on your space and getting in the way of your life. Telling him your feelings straight out will probably solve the problem.

If it doesn't, he's being truly obnoxious about this. The only thing I can think of to do at that point is to completely ignore him. That way you won't be giving him any attention at all—not even the negative attention of telling him to get lost. Hang up when he calls you on the phone; don't say a single word to him when he waits for you after class; get a girlfriend to walk home with you so you can carry on a conversation with her that doesn't include him. In other words just pretend he's not there, and pretty soon he won't be!

Dear Jill,

I've gotten myself into a mess and I don't know how to get out of it. A boy asked me to the big dance at school and I said yes. But then another boy who I really like asked me to the same dance! I didn't know he was going to ask me and I'd *much* rather go with him, but I don't know how to get out of the first date. Is there some way I can go with the boy I like?

Holly F.

Dear Holly,

You've got a really tough problem. And I know exactly how you feel. You want to do what's fair so you can think of yourself as a nice person. But another part of you is saying, "Forget that first guy, I want to have a good time and I know I'll have more fun with the second guy." Unfortunately I'm afraid that there is no really good solution.

You can always try some sort of elaborate scheme, like telling the first guy that your cousin is coming into town and you don't want to leave her home alone so would he take her and then you'll go with the second guy and the four of you can double-date. If guy number one falls for this, then all you'll need to do is find a girl from a different school to pretend to be your cousin, and you're all set. But of course, this first guy is sure to say "No problem. I've got a friend for your cousin, and he can take her." And any other plan you dream up is likely to have similar problems.

I guess you'll have to make a choice here. If you don't mind offending the first guy, you can say, "Look, I know I said I'd go with you, but Joe asked me too, and I'd rather go with him." You'll be able to go with the guy you like better, but the first guy will probably never speak to you again. And he's right. You did accept his offer, and it's not very nice to unaccept when you get an offer you like better. I'm sure your mother would say you've got to grit your teeth and go with the first guy because that's the right thing to do. But there's nothing to stop you from letting the second guy know that you wish you could go with him and you hope he'll ask you out some other time.

Chapter 6

Making the Most of What You've Got

PEOPLE SOMETIMES ASK me if I wear makeup all the time. The answer is no. If I'm just hanging around the house, I usually have on some old sweats and have barely managed to wash my face in the morning, much less put on makeup. Most of my friends don't wear any makeup either if they're just home doing their homework or something like that. Of course, if we're going out, then that's a different story!

But no matter how I'm dressed or whether or not my face is made up, I do care about how I look. I used to think I was really ugly, and nothing anyone said could make me feel any different. At one point I wanted to get a nose job, but now I'm glad I didn't.

I think at some point or another most of us are critical about how we look. There isn't any solution to this problem that I know of. It certainly doesn't help to have some well-meaning adult tell you that you're gorgeous, especially if you know it isn't so. I remember looking at photos of myself and thinking, Wow, what a fat little baby face. I guess what happens is that finally you get used to how you look and learn to make the most of it. At least I think that's what happened to me.

WISHING FOR WHAT YOU HAVEN'T GOT

I've always looked young for my age and I've always been small as well. It never seemed fair to me! My dad is real tall, and both Chuck and Nancy are tall too. Nancy is five eight! But I'm average like my mom. I'm only five feet four and a half inches. So naturally I wanted to be taller and look older. In junior high I could never find clothes that looked grown-up enough on me. I felt I always looked like a little kid.

I remember once when I went clothes shopping with a girlfriend. At that time I was about four feet ten and she was almost five eight. We wanted to get matching clothes, but anything she could wear looked totally dumb on me. I was ready to cry. Then the most embarrassing thing happened. We went to a hamburger place, and some guys came over and said to her, "Let us know when you get rid of your little sister." I wanted to crawl into a hole! She thought it was pretty funny, and so did my mom when I told her the story. My mom told me that I'd be happy to have a young-looking face when I got older. She still tells me that!

One of the things we all worry about is our figures. At least I do. When I was younger, I was so flat-chested that I thought I looked like a boy. And it didn't help any when my mom caught me stuffing my bra with Kleenex! But the funny thing was that only a couple of years later I got into this totally embarrassing situation because my figure had finally filled out. We were on location in Australia, shooting in a church. The *Love Boat* episodes that were showing on television there were about two years old, so people in Australia had only seen me on television as a little kid. This nine-year-old boy came in to watch some of the shooting and when he saw me he said in this real loud voice, "Look, she's got boobs!" I guess you can't win.

Now that I'm older, I've learned to accept how I look and try to make the most of my best features. Some things have never mattered much to me. I figure freckles are freckles, and I've never cared that I get them when I've been out in the sun. I'd still like to be five eight instead of five four and have long thin legs, but I don't really want to change me. It's important to be happy with the way you are, with who you are. I think you've got to have respect for yourself if you want to feel more self-confident.

My main problem now is weight. I gain weight easily, and it's hard to take it off. I always make a joke about it and tell people, "I'm not overweight, I'm just undertall." But it really does bother me. And it's important that I stay slim, not just for my own feelings about how I look, but for my work as well. The camera makes everyone look about ten pounds heavier than they really are.

It's easy to let those extra pounds sneak up on you. You get used to the way you look in the mirror, and I guess that since you see yourself every day, your eyes adjust to that little bit more of yourself that smiles back at you. Then one day you put on your favorite jeans, and you can't get them to zip even if you lie on the floor! That's when you know that it's time to go on a diet.

YOU ARE WHAT YOU EAT

When I started on my diet, I went to a doctor and got his recommendations. I felt that that was important. After all, I'm not a nutritionist. He gave me a list of what to have at each meal so that I'd get a balanced diet and still lose weight. I still go to him every week. He checks my weight, but he also makes sure that I'm eating properly. It's not a good idea just to pick a diet out of a magazine or something without checking first with a doctor to make sure it's the right diet for you.

My diet includes a lot of chicken and fish and steamed vegetables. It's lucky for me that I like those things. But even if you have good intentions, it's often hard to stick to a diet. I have to go to a lot of fancy charity dinners as part of my job, so I always ask if they have a vegetable plate or some plain chicken or fish. Even that doesn't always work. Not too long ago at one of these dinners I asked for a diet plate and what they gave me was three pieces of fried chicken. That delicious deep-fried coating is just packed with calories. It wasn't easy to peel off every bit of the skin and coating, but I knew that if I ate that chicken the way it came I'd gained back every ounce I'd lost that week.

I have to be strict about my diet. Right at the beginning I learned that I can't take "just one bite" of the things I love, like ice cream and chocolate bars and chocolate chip cookies. If I do, it's all over. I have found that for me it really is easier not to have any at all.

It's harder to stick to a diet when you eat in restaurants. One trick I learned was to skip those get-togethers with relatives and friends that center around food and to invite them over to the house after the meal instead. Then I can eat the breakfast I'm supposed to and not be tempted to have waffles with syrup or something like that. Another thing I do is keep lots of sugarless gum and diet soft drinks around. That way when I want to put something in my mouth, there's stuff handy that won't do my diet any damage. The only thing you've got to be careful of when you've got gum in your mouth is looking like a cow chewing her cud!

One thing I discovered when I went on my diet is that I enjoy fixing my own food. It's kind of fun to get it all ready and to arrange it on the plate so it looks like you're eating more than you are. I've learned to take a longer time to eat, chewing everything more slowly and taking little bites. I think it helps me feel more satisfied with my meals.

Another trick that works for me is to put notes to myself on the refrigerator door reminding me that what I put in my mouth that minute will be with me in the form of fat for a long time. And I have a bunch of snapshots of my thin self that I've taped to the refrigerator door. For me it's important to have a real picture of how I want to look. It helps me stick to my diet even when I don't want to.

SEE JILL JUMP!

Everyone says that it's crucial to exercise when you're dieting, and I think that's true—at least for me. Exercise makes me feel more alert and actually makes me less hungry. And besides, I feel so virtuous after exercising that I don't want to ruin it all by overeating. There's usually a dance class at the studio during lunchtime, and I try to take it. Of course, when I was still in school, I didn't have the time because I had to spend it with my set teacher. Now I belong to a gym and I go there several times a week. I like dance and ballet classes, but I'm not crazy about aerobics and all that jumping around.

I think you should do what feels good to you. After all, you're the one who's doing the exercising, and the more you can enjoy it, the more you're likely to keep it up. I have an exercise bike at home, and I thought that would work out great, but I found that I had more fun at the gym. I like having other people around to supervise. I just switch on my Walkman and try to forget that I'm sweating off all that fat!

Once I'd finally lost some weight, I treated myself to a whole new look. I got a haircut and some new clothes. I think it helps to reward yourself for losing inches and pounds, even if you haven't quite reached the ideal you. Your reward doesn't have to be clothes. It can be a record or a tape you've been wanting or those earrings you've been dying to have. The important thing is to figure out what will work for you and to save some money so you can give yourself a treat.

HAIR—YOUR CROWNING GLORY

I change my hairstyle fairly often because I get tired of it being the same way all the time and I like to keep up with the trends. My hair is blond, but it's got reddish highlights that show up in the summer from the sun, so if I don't want it to look too red, I have to keep it covered when I'm out on the beach all day. A while ago I had it cut into a bob, but then I got a shorter cut. One thing you can count on is that your hair will grow out no matter what you do with it.

The short cut I have now is quite versatile. I can tease

up the top and slick back the sides with gel. My idea of a good haircut is one that gives me a chance to have a bunch of different looks without a whole lot of effort. That way I can be creative and express how I feel without doing anything drastic. I sometimes wonder if I'd try something weird like putting a green streak in my hair or letting a tail grow down the back if I weren't on *The Love Boat*. But that kind of far-out style wouldn't go very well with the character I play, so I guess I'll never know.

I like being able to decide how my hair is going to be cut. The way I have it now is great. It's so easy to take care of, I do it myself for the show most of the time. I wash it every day in the shower and I often use some mousse. I like mousse—it really works. It's like setting lotion, only not so heavy. It shapes my hair and helps make it do what I want it to. Then I blow-dry my hair and use a round brush. Sometimes I get out the curling iron for finishing touches.

Taking care of my hair myself lets me find the look I like. When I was little, I was a swimmer and my mom had my hair permed in an Afro because it was the easiest way for her to manage it. But I hated it that way. I thought it was a terrible look for me.

I guess the good thing about being responsible for things like doing your own hair is that you get a chance to do it the way you want. Sometimes it takes a while to find a style that looks good on you. But it's fun to experiment and try out different looks.

FIXING YOUR FACE

Until we were about fourteen, my friends and I didn't wear makeup. Sometimes, though, things got a little confusing for me because I had to wear it on the show. I was used to seeing myself in full makeup, including base. One time I almost made a total fool of myself. I had stopped at my girlfriend's house on the way to school, and when she came to the door, she gave me a funny look. I suddenly realized that I had absentmindedly put on full makeup as if I was going to the studio. I ran into her bathroom and washed my face. If

I'd gone to school like that, I'd never have heard the end of it!

I still don't wear much makeup when I'm going somewhere during the day, unless I'm working on the show. But when I'm going out for the evening or on a date, I have a whole routine. My mom says it takes me hours to get ready, but I'm sure it doesn't take nearly as long as she thinks. After all, all I do is take a shower, blow-dry my hair, curl it, do my makeup, and get dressed.

But I must admit that when I put on makeup, I'm really picky. I guess that's something I picked up from the makeup people on the show. I put a base on and make sure it's all even. In my house that's not easy. I have terrible light in my bathroom, and I end up running from mirror to mirror all over the house to make sure it's on evenly. Next I put on contour and rouge and then I work on my eyes. I use eyeliner and eyeshadow, usually in two different shades so I can highlight the area just below my eyebrows. And of course, I never get around to plucking my eyebrows until right before I go out, even though I know I should do it some other time. Then I put on mascara and curl my eyelashes. I finish up with lipstick and lip liner and lip gloss. Now that I think about it, Mom is probably right—it takes me quite a while!

As my character on the show gets more grown up, she gets to wear more makeup. I've noticed that as I wear more makeup in the show I tend to use more in my personal life. I guess I get used to seeing myself that way.

Vicki is really a pretty wholesome type. She isn't supposed to look glamorous, so I've never had a chance to try out the "femme fatale" look. Sometimes I wish I could make myself up to look like some of those supersexy ladies, but then I figure it's really not me. I don't think makeup works to make you look like someone you're not. It's just supposed to make who you are look better.

Taking off makeup correctly is almost as important as putting it on the right way. At least that's what the makeup people on the show say. So I try really hard to take my makeup off every night before I go to bed. I wash my face and then use an astringent and then put on eye cream. And I'm always gentle with the soft skin under my eyes and I try to remember to stroke upward on my neck and cheeks. They say that's to keep you from getting wrinkles when you get older. But sometimes I get lazy and I don't take off all my eyeliner. Then I wake up in the morning looking like I've been up all night with big dark circles under my eyes. My mom says I look like a raccoon, and I guess it isn't very attractive.

I know I'm not supposed to pick at my face, but sometimes I just can't help myself. I've got it down almost to a science, even though I think it's pretty gross. Luckily I haven't done any real damage, and at the studio—once they've put on my base—it doesn't even show. But it's one bad habit I've decided to stop!

SOAKING UP THE SUN

Because *The Love Boat* takes place on a cruise ship, I'm supposed to look fairly tan all year. In the summer it's no problem. I tan easily, and I like looking tan. Besides, going to the beach is social time and I really enjoy it. People tell me that I should be careful about being out in the sun because it's supposed to be bad for the skin and I'll get wrinkles. But I figure that I can't worry about every little thing! If I have wrinkles when I'm sixty or so, I'll just get a facelift! I do try not to get my face too tan though. It's easier for the makeup people when my face isn't too brown.

In the winter getting a tan isn't so easy. Even here in Southern California the winter sun isn't strong enough unless I lie out in it forever. And I don't have the time to do that. Sometimes I use the tanning rooms at my gym, but usually I just don't worry about it.

THE FINISHING TOUCH

My nails need to look nice for the show, and I want them to look good for the rest of the time. I like a fairly natural look. That works well for my character and for my personal life as well. I often get red nail polish for the Christmas show, but most of the time I get a French manicure. That's the kind where the tip of your nail is painted white both on top and underneath and then your whole fingernail is covered with a sort of natural-looking pearly polish.

I've tried doing my own French manicure, but I always get the edge of the white part all squiggly. I guess I don't have enough patience to do it right. If I didn't have to get professional manicures for the show, I think I'd ask a friend to do it for me. Lots of girls I know do their own manicures, and it looks as good as if they'd been to the beauty parlor and had it done.

My own nails aren't very strong. When they get long, they peel or start to break. I tried drinking gelatin but it didn't work for me. Maybe I didn't do it long enough. Anyway, what I do now is have my nails filed so that the ends are sort of squared off. I find that pointy nails tend to break a lot faster than squared off or rounded ones. And I get a light coat of acrylic on top of my nails to give them strength and to make my manicures last longer. That way my polish doesn't seem to chip too much, and I can go three weeks between manicures.

I think that however you look as far as your makeup and hair and nails go is really a reflection of who you are. It's important that you choose a look that fits into your lifestyle and is easy to maintain. For instance, if you are involved in sports almost every day, you probably shouldn't try to do your hair in an elaborate style that takes a lot of time. Or if you love to work in the garden or develop your own photographs, you'll be better off with shorter nails and clear polish that won't show the chips so quickly.

Spending a whole lot of time trying to look like your idea of someone else doesn't get you anywhere. And besides, it's no fun. Part of the reason I feel about this the way I do is probably because I was raised in a home where looking natural has always been the thing to do. And I'm sure that the kind of character I play on *The Love Boat* also influences how I look at things. I do think looking your best is important, and that means looking like the uniquely wonderful person you really are.

YOUR OWN SPACE

Having a place where you can go off and be by yourself is great. We teenagers often feel the need to get away from the rest of the family and just think things over all on our own. There are times when I like to close my door and shut out the world for a little while.

I'm lucky that I have my own room, and I really love it. I've been able to fix it up just the way I want. It's got pretty carpet in a dusty rose, and the walls are covered with old-fashioned print paper in tones of blue and cream. I found matching fabric for the ruffled curtains and bedspread so it all kind of goes together. My brass bed is loaded with lots of pillows, and I love to sit there and watch TV. (I tell Mom that I have to watch TV—it's part of my job!)

I'm a collector of all kinds of things, and anyone who walked into my room could tell a lot about me just by looking around. My doll collection, which I started a long time ago, is still on display, and so are all my bears, which is my other big collection. I have a huge wicker hamper full of stuffed bears, and then I have a bunch of others, like wooden ones from different countries and a little porcelain one to wear around my neck. My shelves are covered with mementos from my trips—little wooden boxes, picture frames made of shells, and glass figurines.

Of course, I have millions of photos. One whole table is covered with framed ones of my family and friends and people I've worked with, and I have a whole set of Polaroids I took of the *Love Boat* cast and crew. As you can imagine, I'm running out of space! I've promised myself that some day soon I'm going to move the loose photos into these pretty albums with eyelet covers that I got for my birthday. But I haven't done it yet!

Another thing I love is jewelry. I have a whole boxful of earrings, and I have a great time picking out which ones to wear every day. In fact, I thought about getting a second hole pierced in my ears—that way I could wear more earrings! But my mom said absolutely not. And after a while I decided she was right. You know how some older women sometimes have a line on their earlobes going down from the earring hole? Well, I thought one on each ear is bad enough and how ugly it would be to have two of them!

I HAVEN'T GOT A THING TO WEAR!

How many times have you said that? And your mom always says, "Don't be silly, you've got a whole closetful of clothes!"

I have that same conversation all the time. And it's true, I do have a closetful of clothes. But sometimes I feel the need for something brand-new!

As you know, I love shopping. I'm lucky because I often have a good excuse to buy something new, since I go to a lot of dressy affairs because of my work. I do try to be careful about how much I spend, though, and I watch for the sales. Clothes are incredibly expensive. It's fun to try things on even if I don't plan to buy them. Sometimes I go to the wardrobe department at the studio and try on a whole lot of different outfits. It's a good way of testing what looks good on me and finding my best look. I think I've figured out what shades go best with my skin and hair tones.

When I was younger, I worried a lot about what to wear every day. It was important to look with-it and in style. Then I went to a high school where we were required to wear uniforms. You'd think that would take all the pressure off how to dress. In a way it did, but after a while we all tried to cheat a little bit on the uniform code. We'd wear polo shirts under our sweaters instead of regular blouses, and I don't think I wore my blazer more than a couple of times—it was always stuffed in the bottom of my locker.

Now I think of my clothes as being in two different categories—regular and dress-up. I have more dress-up clothes than most girls because of my work. It's so much fun to pick them out. I don't buy something new for every occasion though—I can't get away with that! Mom made a rule that I have to wear each formal dress at least five times. That's okay with me. I love to get dressed up, and I'll probably wear some of them a lot more often than that. For instance, I have this gorgeous dress I got for my Senior Prom which I adore. I've already worn it to several other occasions.

Besides, I never throw anything away! That's one of my problems, I guess. It's embarrassing if anyone looks into my closet—it's so jammed full of stuff that it's hard to find anything. And I've got so many pairs of shoes because I can't bear to get rid of them, even when they're all scuffed and beat up.

I keep telling myself that I have to go through my closet and weed out the things I don't wear anymore, but somehow that hasn't happened yet. I'll have to do it soon though—it's getting to be too messy even for me! And I have to admit that I don't put things away as neatly as I should. One time I had left a pair of pantyhose on the floor after I took them off, and one of my dogs dragged it out into the middle of the living room floor—right while my mom was having a big party! I was mortified! Maybe someday I'll learn to prevent these embarrassing moments before they happen.

Dear Jill,

I've done something that I now know was pretty dumb but I don't know what to do about it. A while back I thought it would be great to have the punk look, so I cut my hair real short and dyed it bright orange. Well, you can probably guess how I feel about it now. Is there anything I can do to get rid of my punk mistake?

Penny G.

Dear Penny,

There is really no way for you to get back your old hairstyle instantly unless you spend a lot of money on a wig! What I suggest is that you talk to a professional hairstylist and get his or her advice. I'm sure your hair can be redyed so at least the color will look like it used to, and in a couple of months it will have grown out enough so that you can have it trimmed in an attractive cut. Meanwhile, just admit to the world, "Okay, so I was dumb. I won't do it again!"

You sound like someone who loves to wear the latest

styles. Have you considered wearing hats for a while and setting a trend of your own?

Dear Jill,

I hate the way I look. My ears stick out and I can't stand it. Please don't tell me that it's all just my imagination or that I look cute the way I am—that's what my parents say, and it doesn't help. It's not my imagination. Can anyone help me?

Roberta S.

Dear Roberta,

I know your problem is really bothering you, and I think the most obvious solution is to have a hairstyle that covers your ears. Go to a good hair salon and tell them your problem. It's worth spending the extra money to get a look that makes you feel pretty.

If you haven't already done this, give it a try. You'll be amazed at what a terrific haircut can do for your looks. After a while you may forget all about your ears. I know it's not your imagination, but other people see the whole you and don't focus on the one slightly imperfect part. And after you've looked in your mirror for a few months and seen hair—not ears—you probably won't focus on them so much yourself.

If after six months or so, you're still totally crazed about this problem, talk to your parents about cosmetic surgery.

Dear Jill,

I have to wear glasses. I've been to every eye doctor in town, and they all say that I can't wear contacts. But I feel like such a clunk. Is there any way to look glamorous with glasses?

Emily C.

Dear Emily,

Sure, there is! Lots of people who don't even need to, wear sunglasses because they like the look. The big problem is that good-looking frames are expensive. But since it sounds like you wear your glasses all the time, it's probably a worthwhile investment.

Find out where the biggest optical center is near your home. Even if it's in a neighboring town, take the time to go there and see what they've got. Ask a friend whose taste you trust to go with you. And when you get there, try on every kind of frame they have. I know that you and your friend together will be able to find something that not only looks good on you but actually adds to your attractiveness. The saying that "men seldom make passes at girls who wear glasses" hasn't been true for years!

Chapter 7

Good-bye for Now!

WHEN I LOOK back at my early teen years, I realize that some of the problems that loomed so large for me turned out to be not that important. I'm sure you can remember when you were in kindergarten or first grade, and you said, "I won't be your friend anymore if you don't let me ride your bike!" That sounds kind of silly now, and you probably can't believe you were so upset about something so trivial. And now you know that friendship is based on more lasting things than a bike ride.

In the same way you'll probably find in a few years that the crises you're going through right now will look unimportant or even funny. I think this process goes on all through people's lives. When we're all grandmothers, we'll look back and say, "How silly I was to get so upset about that when I was twenty." But of course, we'll be worrying then about the problems of growing old!

I don't mean to say that the problems of the teen years

aren't important ones. They are, and we have to find our own ways of dealing with them before we can move on to the next stage of our lives. But it does help to know that we will get through these often troubled times.

It seems to me that one of the issues that teenage girls worry about most is popularity. We're always wondering: Am I popular? How can I be more popular? What's wrong with me if I'm not invited to parties with the popular crowd? And a lot of our concerns about our looks and about getting along with boys reflect our fears and insecurities about being popular.

I was thinking about this the other day, and I got out my yearbook from junior high. It was amazing to look at the pictures and to remember who were the really popular girls back then. Sometimes I envied them so much. But it's strange. Now a lot of those girls are at the back of the crowd, while many of the kids who weren't real social and popular in those days are the leaders today.

Of course, none of us wants to try to be out of it in junior high so we can be real successful later on! And it doesn't make you any less unhappy when you're sitting home on Saturday night to know that in a few years you may have more dates than you can handle. You want answers to your questions right now, and the *Just for Us* books are written with that in mind. But sometimes when you're really miserable, it helps to say to yourself that things will be better later on.

There is one terrible event in my life that I like to remember now because it had an interesting ending. A community theater near where I was living was putting on a musical and I wanted to be in it. I had been in a number of other shows at theaters around Livermore, and I thought I had a good chance of getting a part in this one because in this particular show there were a lot of parts for children.

There was a man on the board of the theater who wanted his daughter to be in the show. It wasn't any problem as far as I could see—there were plenty of kids' parts, and we could both have been in it. But he didn't see it that way. Maybe he felt that since I'd been in other plays, I'd hog the limelight or something. Anyway, he called the director and said I couldn't play any part at all in the production. If I did, he'd close down the theater and lock out the whole cast.

The director was a really nice man, and he was upset about this, but there wasn't anything he could do about it. He explained the whole situation to me, and I was crushed. I had been looking forward to being in the show so much! Finally I asked if I could be an usher or something, and he said that was fine.

On the night the show opened, they let me put on a costume and go out in front to hand out programs. I was happy to be there at all, and I was standing by the door through which the audience was entering when the man from the theater board came in.

He looked furious when he saw me, and he told me I had no business being out in the lobby in costume. He ordered me to go back to the green room, which is the place backstage where the actors wait when they're not onstage. I tried to explain why I was there, but he wouldn't listen. He grabbed my arm and pushed me through the door and down the stairs toward the back of the stage.

I was so scared! If I hadn't grabbed the railing, I might have really gotten hurt, but luckily I didn't. I was crying, and I couldn't understand why he was so mad at me. Of course, my parents came to get me. They wanted to leave right away and never set foot in the place again. But I wanted to stay and see my friends in the show.

In case you're wondering if the interesting ending I was talking about was that I got to play one of the children in the show, that's not what happened! In fact, after that incident my parents thought seriously of not letting me be in acting at all if I would have to deal with such horrible people.

But within the next three months everything broke open for me, and I started my career in television. It really made me believe that when one door closes, another one opens.

Many times all of us feel that everything is going wrong, and we'll never get our lives going in the direction we want. Of course, luck can play a big part in everyone's life. Things can start to go right again for no reason you can see. But I think we have to do our best to help ourselves. All of us can make the best of what we have. If you dwell on what's wrong with your life at the moment, you just sink deeper and deeper into feeling sorry for yourself. But if you look hard enough for that silver lining, sooner or later you'll find it—or in the looking, you'll find a way to make your own.

Watch for

SELF-CONFIDENCE
SUPER HAIR
BEING FRIENDS

next in the JUST FOR US series
from Pinnacle Books

coming in November!

AND

MEETING BOYS
MAKE YOURSELF BEAUTIFUL
FALLING IN LOVE

Coming in January!